Vicki Johnson was the head teacher of an outstanding primary school for many years. Throughout her career, she wrote specifically for groups of children, adapting plots and characters to reflect their interests and devising scripts, musicals and stories to inspire, engage and challenge. She began writing thrillers for reluctant readers but which could also be read aloud and hold the attention of everyone in a class. With *Wolf Jacket*, even reluctant teenage boys have been known to read ahead. Married, with two grown-up children and four grandchildren, she lives in Exmouth, Devon.

Dedication

To Kim, who always thought that I *could*; Rosie, Dave, Sam and Mel who agreed that I *should*; and Evie, Matilda, Arthur and Sid for whom I *did*.

Northwood Primary School children inspired me to start writing, and Pie Corbett thought I should keep going. The children of the following schools agreed: Honiton Primary School, Marpool Primary School, Exeter Road Community Primary School, Charlotte Turner Primary School, and Croesyceiliog Secondary School. I'm grateful to them all.

Vicki Johnson

WOLF JACKET

AUSTIN MACAULEY PUBLISHERS™

LONDON • CAMBRIDGE • NEW YORK • SHARJAH

A CIP catalogue record for this title is available from the British Library.

ISBN 9781788482189 (Paperback)
ISBN 9781788482196 (Hardback)
ISBN 9781788482202 (E-Book)

www.austinmacauley.com

First Published (2018)
Austin Macauley Publishers Ltd™
25 Canada Square
Canary Wharf
London
E14 5LQ

Chapter One

He needed a wee.

He was squashed up against the window of the train next to his big brother Nate. The man in a suit opposite him had his case on the floor under a shared table, and he'd have to somehow climb over it, squeeze past Nate and the knees of the two fat ladies across the aisle.

'I need a wee,' he hissed to Nate.

'Why didn't you go before we got on?' said Nate irritably.

'I didn't want to go then, did I?' He crossed his legs. 'And now I do, *badly.*'

'Well, get going then,' said Nate without looking up from his music magazine.

'What, by myself?'

'Well, I can't go *for* you!' said Nate, a bit too loudly for the boy's liking. 'Unless you want me to wipe your bum?'

'I'll go on my own then,' he said, expecting Nate to say he'd come too, but he didn't.

The boy eased himself over the briefcase and fell across the table as the train lurched round a bend.

'Steady on, Lesley!' said the man in the suit.

'My name's not Lesley,' said the boy, trying to regain his balance. 'It's Mitch.'

Nate rolled his eyes at the man in the suit as if to say 'What can I tell you? He's ten!'

He pulled out a card from his jacket.

'Take your ticket,' Nate said. 'Just in case you see a ticket inspector or something.'

Which was, he later realised, a big mistake.

Mitch took the ticket and followed the signs for the toilet. It seemed a long way. As he walked along the corridor, through hissing doors which slid open and shut, all the passengers looked up briefly, and then back down at their phones.

No one asked to see his ticket.

The toilet gurgled and squeaked alarmingly even if you didn't press anything, which Mitch didn't. He imagined being sucked by some invisible force through the stainless steel hole and onto the tracks.

It was weird; swaying, wobbling and weeing all at once.

He had trouble washing his hands. *What did you have to do to get water?* Looking around he saw a rubber pad on the floor. He stood on it and water gushed into the sink, all over his trousers. Great. Now everyone would think he had wet himself. He was trying to dry his trousers with the hand dryer when the train stopped.

Mitch heaved back the door and saw they were at a station.

They couldn't be there already, could they? Usually, it took ages to get to Portsmouth, but then that was when they were with Dad. Being with Nate for the first time on their own had felt like much more of a challenge, even a bit scary; things always went faster if they were exciting, just like Mr Barry said when they were learning about "time". Mr Barry had asked which was longer, assembly or break. Mitch could not believe that they were the same.

He looked out of the window and saw that the train was certainly at a station. Was it Portsmouth Harbour? There were so many people on the platform, getting on or off the train, it was hard to see anything other than bodies. There should be a sign hanging up somewhere with the name of the station surely.

And then, Mitch saw Nate. He was pushing his way through the crowds towards the ticket barrier.

The doors hissed shut.

'Wait!' shouted Mitch. 'I've got to get off!'

'Steady on, Lesley!' It was that man again. 'Don't panic!'

He was waiting to go to the toilet that Mitch had just left. 'Press that button, *then* panic!'

Hilarious, thought Mitch, but the doors opened again and he jumped down onto the platform just as the stationmaster blew his whistle.

Normally Mitch would have watched the train pull away; he used to have all the Thomas the Tank Engine books and secretly wished he could still watch the DVDs he pretended were babyish. Now though, he needed to catch up with Nate. He ran up to the barrier and saw the back of Nate's jacket, on the other side.

'Nate! Nathan! Wait!'

It was noisy and Nate didn't hear, and he didn't stop. Instead, he turned left at the station door, and disappeared out of sight.

Mitch fumbled for the ticket Nate had given him "*just in case*".

He wasn't sure what to do with it so he stood back and watched as several passengers fed their cards into the ticket machines and walked through the padded one-way gates.

Mitch did the same. The ticket disappeared, the gates opened and he followed the crowd out of the station. He took a minute to look about him. Nothing looked familiar.

A sickening thought occurred to him; the train had left the station, hadn't it? *It had carried on down a track.* They couldn't be at Portsmouth Harbour then, because after the Harbour there was nothing but sea. So why had Nate got off? There was only one thing to do now: keep up with Nate and see what the flipping heck he was playing at.

'Nate!' Mitch saw the back of his brother just turning a corner. He put two fingers in his mouth and did their special whistle, the one Dad had taught them. Several people turned and stared but Nate carried on.

Mitch hurtled along the road feeling a familiar restriction beginning to spread across his chest. He fumbled in his pocket for his inhaler. He must have left it in his bag. That was a point! Had Nate picked up his bag? And what about his top? He must have, he wouldn't just leave all his stuff on a train surely. There was Dad's phone he was supposed to be looking after, and the sausage and bacon baguette he was saving for later.

He knew he'd have to stop for a moment and not "get in a state" as Dad would say. He leant against the wall and tried to control his breathing. His eyes were watering and he wiped them with the back of his hand.

A man was standing in front of him.

'Are you in need of assistance?'

The man had thick hair, matted into long curls, which fell over his shoulders and across most of his face. *Yuk! Skanky*, thought Mitch.

'May I help?'

The man put down the Big Issue magazines he was selling and fumbled in his pocket. His voice wasn't quite right somehow, almost posh, as if he'd got the wrong body like in a game of Heads, Body, Legs.

'Have one of these, old chap,' said the skanky man, holding out a tube of silver foil-wrapped sweets.

They looked grubby, fluffy from a dirty pocket and Mitch could smell something sharp and sour that reminded him of the toilet on the train.

He remembered a film he'd seen at his mate Jason's house about a boy who'd got lost in a wood, and how a wizard, pretending to be friendly, offered him a delicious looking drink which was poisoned, obviously! Duh! He and Jason had shouted at the boy not to drink it. They'd thought he was stupid to fall for a trick like that.

'No you're alright,' said Mitch. 'Cheers,' he added, not wanting to be rude, but edging away as fast as he could. 'I'm with my brother. He's really big.'

Mitch felt stupid saying this as Nate wasn't really that big, but he didn't want the man to think he was on his own, just in case. He jogged down the hill, glad to get away from the man with the hair and anxious to catch up with Nate. Ha! He was there, just crossing that road and going into a shop.

'Gotcha!' muttered Mitch. At last! He felt a wave of relief; Nate was in that shop. All Mitch had to do was cross the road and then he'd give him such an earache for making him run like this and get all wheezy.

The traffic was heavy in both directions, two lanes on each side. He'd have to cross half way and wait for a gap. He was tall for a ten-year-old, but even so, it was hard to see over the cars as well as keeping an eye on the shop, in case Nate came out. He got half-way and stood ready to race across onto the other side.

There was a gap, he stepped out...and straight into the path of a cyclist.

Chapter Two

All Mitch remembered later was a screech, a bang, a scream and a groan; he wasn't sure in what order. He remembered seeing the cyclist lying on the road inches away from the wheels of a van, the bike's wheels spinning upside down in the air. There were car doors opening all around as people got out of their vehicles to see what was going on; one man was on his phone ringing for an ambulance.

'What the bloody hell were you doing, running into the road like that, you stupid moron?'

The van driver was leaning out of his window and yelling, his face huge with anger.

'Do you want to get yourself killed? Haven't you got eyes in your thick head?'

The cyclist groaned again and tried to sit up. Mitch backed away. The traffic was at a standstill. He should run, get as far as possible from the shouting van driver and the blood pouring down the cyclist's face.

'Oi! You little toe-rag, I'm talking to you.'

The van driver was coming towards him now. 'See what you've done? This is all your fault!'

Mitch looked around at the muddle of traffic, at the queue, which was already tailing back as far as he could see. He heard angry horns competing with the van driver's furious shouts. He looked past them all for Nate to come out of the shop and rescue him, saw the shop door open and someone wearing Nate's jacket came out.

It was Nate's jacket, but the person wearing it wasn't Nate.

Mitch felt giddy and sort of sick. This was a mess. He'd made a shocking mistake. Someone was wearing Nate's jacket so who? And how? He needed to think, to sort it out, but not with the van driver shouting and the car horns blaring and certainly not with the cyclist beginning to thrash about with blood still pouring from his head, groping for support and moaning in pain.

'I'm sorry!' Mitch said.

As he spoke, he squeezed through a gap in the stationary cars, holding up his hands as if in surrender.

'I didn't mean it. I'm careful normally, honest I am. I'm sorry.'

He kept talking and walking and moving further and further away until he could see enough space to run fast, as fast as he'd ever run before, ignoring the wheeze, which was beginning to choke his lungs and tighten his chest, ignoring the stitch, which was gripping his side.

He risked a glance over his shoulder to see if the van driver was chasing him, lost his footing, made windmills of his arms trying to regain his balance and fell forwards into a concrete bus stop.

Mitch really did see stars; they exploded in and around his head. For a second he couldn't focus. He picked himself up and tried to stand without stumbling. He could feel a lump pushing up through the stubble on his head. He wasn't sure if he was bleeding.

'Hello again! You still about? Not looking too clever though if you'll forgive my saying so.'

It was the skanky man, the wizard, the one with the poisoned sweets.

He was sitting on a bench by the bus stop, a cardboard cup of something hot in one hand, and a piece of string in the other. There was no sign of the magazines he had been selling. Mitch was still feeling dizzy but he managed to make out that the piece of string was attached to a red scarf tied round the neck of a large dog.

'Let me introduce you to Red,' said the wizard. 'He won't hurt, I assure you. Any friend of mine is a friend of yours, eh Red?'

The dog thumped a brush of a tail on the floor, wiping the dirt from side to side.

'I got a headache.' said Mitch in a faint voice. Saying the word "headache" made him want Dad or even Nate.

'You've got a lump the size of a kumquat on your head to go with it,' said the wizard.

'Can you see?' asked Mitch, not liking the sound of a kumquat. 'Is it bad?'

'I can, and it's not life-threatening. I've seen worse that's for sure.'

He fumbled in one of his many pockets and bought out a triangle of plastic with a sandwich cut neatly to fit inside. He tore off the edge of the plastic and pulled it out, releasing an oniony cheesy smell. He gave half to Red and held out the rest to Mitch.

'Want a bite?' he asked.

'No, you're alright,' replied Mitch shaking his head, his stomach still churning from the accident.

'So, what's the situation my young friend?'

Mitch tried to think.

'Well, to be honest I can't really work it out. I mean half an hour back there wasn't any *"situation"*. Me and my brother Nate, we were just on a train.'

'What train?' asked the wizard.

'The train from London, you know? Where Nan lives. We've never done it before. Not on our own.'

Mitch looked at his feet and felt the wheeze tightening.

'I see,' said the wizard. 'You said were on the train?'

'Yeah. Going home. Me and Nate.'

'Is that so?' said the wizard. 'And where precisely is home?'

'Ventnor. It's on the Isle of Wight.'

'Is it? Is it really?' said the wizard. He was staring hard. It made Mitch feel uncomfortable, like when he'd told Mr

Barry it wasn't him who'd blocked the drain in the playground, when it actually was.

Mitch rubbed at the kumquat growing on his head.

'My head really kills.'

'Go on though,' said the wizard. 'I like a good story. You were on the way home and…?'

'I went to the toilet,' said Mitch glumly. 'I should've waited, or gone at Waterloo before I got on the train, like Nate said.'

'No, sorry, not making any sense at all. How have you got from the lavvy on the train to a bus shelter in Guildford with a bruise the size of a clementine…'

'I thought you said kumquat?' interrupted Mitch anxiously feeling his forehead.

'Kumquat, clementine. Do go on.'

'I was on the train and then Nate, my brother, got off, so I did too, only it wasn't Nate.'

Mitch suddenly realised something for the very first time: Nate was still on the train with absolutely no idea what had happened.

'Nate's going to be really mad. And Dad; he'll go bonkers.'

'But your mum won't mind?' the wizard asked quizzically.

Mitch kicked at the floor. 'Mum's gone.'

There was a pause.

'Ah!'

'Dad'll never let us get the train again, not on our own,' said Mitch.

He looked down at his fingers as if he was counting.

'We won't get to see Nan, not nearly as much.

'That cyclist is probably bleeding to death.

'I put the ticket Nate gave me, just in case, in the ticket thingy and it never came out which means I can't get back on the train.

'I've got all kinds of exotic fruit growing on my head to go with a thumping headache.

'My wheeze is bad and my inhaler's on the train and that, Mr Wizard, is the situation.'

The wizard raised his eyebrows in surprise.

'You know my name?'

Mitch looked embarrassed. 'I didn't, I mean I don't. It just sort of came out.'

'No matter,' said the man called Mr Wizard. 'Time to go!'

As he said this, a green single decker bus pulled in at the kerb and the doors swished open.

'Hop on!' said Mr Wizard, indicating with an expansive gesture that Mitch should jump on board. Mitch hesitated for a moment. He had no phone, no money, and no idea how to get back to Nate, never mind home. Here was a grown-up who wanted to help. Red thrust his wet muzzle into his hand and thumped his tail enthusiastically.

'In your own time, Sonny Jim,' said the bus driver. 'On or off?'

Mitch got on.

Chapter Three

After Mitch had gone to the toilet, Nate stretched himself across Mitch's seat and allowed his elbows to spread. He was reading "Guitar Guys", something Dad would never have bought. It had been great, being allowed to be at Nan's, and even better being allowed to go on their own.

The train picked up speed and Nate, glancing up from his magazine, noticed that there were absolutely no houses to be seen anywhere now that they had left London behind.

The man in the suit leant towards him. 'Won't he need his stuff then, your friend?'

'What? I mean sorry?'

'Your friend...the one with a shaved head?'

'He's my brother,' said Nate.

'Well, your brother then. He'll need his stuff, won't he? His sweater thingy, and his bag?'

'I'm looking after them for him,' said Nate. 'He's gone to the toilet.'

'Yes, of course. It's just that when he got off...'

'What?' Nate stared at the man in the suit, trying to make sense of what he was saying. 'Got off? Got off what?'

'Why, got off the train, of course. He got off at the station. I did wonder. He seemed to be in a bit of a rush. I helped him with the door. I thought it was odd, but he was quite insistent.'

Nate felt the sickeningly familiar rush of anxiety that was never far away, along with the ache in his chest that had grown since Mum left...

'He got off the train?' He repeated the words to himself and looked at the man in the suit hoping he'd misheard him.

'Well yes, as I said...oh dear. Wasn't he supposed to?'

The man looked bewildered as Nate snatched up the pile of belongings on Mitch's seat and raced along the corridor out of sight.

'Look at that!' said one of the fat ladies. 'He's left his magazine behind.'

Nate got to the toilets knowing it was pointless to search there now. What on earth had made Mitch get off the train? He tried to think how many stations they had stopped at since he last saw his brother. The train was slowing down.

'Havant! The next station is Havant.'

I've got to go back, thought Nate.

He got off the train, crossed the railway bridge to the opposite platform and slumped down on a seat, waiting for the very next train back towards London. He tried to think.

Mitch had been desperate to get off the train according to the man in the suit. Why? What could possibly have made him do such a thing? Was he upset? Not particularly, not like when Mum walked out. It was almost two months now. Missing Mum had become part of who they were, part of their daily reality. They were the boys whose mum had walked out and left them. It was how it was. They dealt with it.

Nate felt another twist in his stomach as he realised that there'd be no chance of Dad letting them go up to London again. His first ever opportunity to show Dad he could look after Mitch, take responsibility, and then this happens.

So, come on now, think! Why else would Mitch have left the train? If he wasn't upset, was he scared? Had he done something stupid and didn't want to get into trouble, or had he seen something he wanted at the station? Sweets, perhaps? No that couldn't be, because, of course, his wallet was in his bag. Mitch had nothing with him, nothing at all apart from, bloody hell, his ticket!

And then Nate felt really bad. Up until that moment, he had pictured Mitch sitting waiting patiently at the station for him to come. He'd be cross at first and then he'd give him a hug and tell him it was alright and then they'd phone Dad to say they'd been delayed and that they were on the 5:30 and not to worry.

But Mitch had his ticket; the ticket Nate had given him *just in case*. He could leave the station anytime he wanted; he could be anywhere by now.

The London train from Portsmouth pulled into Havant and Nate got on. He stood by the door, in readiness to jump out as soon as they got back to the station where Mitch had disappeared.

But when the train stopped at Guildford, Nate saw to his dismay that there were many platforms and hundreds of people. He felt really sick now, sick and sweaty.

He forced himself to think calmly. Mitch wasn't here. What to do, what to do?

The click from the arrivals screen made him look up and he noticed a camera. Of course! CCTV! Cameras were all over the place. They'd be able to track Mitch down in no time at all, surely. He realised that he couldn't do this on his own. He needed help.

***

'You're telling me you've lost your brother.'

The stationmaster and Nate were sitting together in the stationmaster's office.

'Not exactly,' said Nate. 'There was a man in our carriage who saw him get off here at this station. I thought I'd find him if I came back. I got off at Havant, soon as I realised, but he's gone.'

The stationmaster picked up the phone.

'Is there someone we should be telling about all of this? I mean, besides the police, of course. What about your mum? Does she know what's going on?'

Nate shook his head miserably. Not Mum. If she'd been like normal mums, they wouldn't be in this mess. If she hadn't upped and left them with no warning, he wouldn't be looking after his flipping brother. He'd be with his mates having a laugh most like. He'd said it before and he was saying it again…it wasn't fair.

'Are you alright son?' asked the stationmaster. 'Did you hear me?'

Nate hadn't.

'I was saying we need to ring your parents. Or have you done that already?'

Nate shook his head. Dad would be out fishing somewhere. And he didn't have his phone because he'd given it to them. He'd said they could borrow it for the weekend, in case of emergencies. Well, this was surely one of those.

The outer office door opened.

Two policemen were shown in. They filled the tiny office and blocked out the light.

'Good afternoon gentlemen,' said one. 'My name's DI Sanders and this is my colleague PC Lee. I understand there's been an incident.'

Nate felt a little calmer at the word "incident". Not kidnapping then, or, [don't even think it] something worse.

'Thanks for coming so quickly,' said the stationmaster. 'It's probably nothing.'

'We got a message that a young lad's gone missing. Is that right?'

The stationmaster nodded towards Nate. 'It's this lad's brother.'

'And you are…?' said DI Sanders.

'I'm Nathan Jackson, Nate. And my brother, he's Mitchel Jackson, and he's only ten.'

'So who was looking after him then?'

'Me.' Nate looked embarrassed.

'And how old are you?'

'I'm fourteen, nearly fifteen as a matter of fact.' It felt stupid to say that. Like a kid, Nathan realised.

'And now, tell me how he disappeared, from the beginning mind.'

PC Lee took out his notebook and began to write down what Nate was saying. When Nate got to the bit about Mitch leaving the train, the policemen and the stationmaster exchanged glances.

'Tell you what, son. Let's get you down to the nick,' said PC Lee. 'We can get all the details sorted out there.'

Chapter Four

Mitch stared miserably at his shadowy reflection in the bus window, and a boy with a shaved head stared miserably back.

Mitch ran his hand around the unfamiliar sensation of bare skin where only three days ago he'd had thick red hair. He wondered what his mum would have said if she'd seen him all bald. She might have laughed. Or perhaps been cross with Nan for doing it, but not with him. She was never cross with him.

The bus stopped without warning in a very dark place. Mitch peered out of the window and could see nothing.

Mr Wizard stood up to get off the bus.

'Chop, chop! We're here.'

Mitch noticed the other passengers were giving them odd looks. Two elderly ladies clucked their disapproval and one whispered 'Shame. Poor little soul.'

Mitch felt his ears reddening as he realised they must be thinking that Mr Wizard was his dad.

They stepped off the bus and Mitch watched as the tail lights of the bus disappeared around the corner of the road. He had a sudden urge to run after it, waving his arms and shouting for help.

It was cold now, and he had nothing but the clothes he'd been wearing when he'd been for a wee back on the train. It seemed like ages ago. He wished he had his hooded green top to keep his newly naked head from freezing.

'Where are we?' said Mitch.

'Here!' said Mr Wizard.

Mr Wizard produced a key from his pocket with a flourish and aimed it at a clump of bushes.

A light winked and bleeped. Parked behind the hedge was a brand-new BMW.

'What's this?' asked Mitch, amazed.

'A car? It's a self-propelled machine designed for domestic passenger use made up of various systems all of which can operate in isolation but whose combined function produces the final vehicle.'

'I know that!' said Mitch. 'I'm not a complete div!'

'I didn't think for one moment you were,' said Mr Wizard.

Mr Wizard undid Red's spotted scarf and string. He stuffed them into a bag and placed the bag in the boot. Red shook himself, and for the first time, Mitch noticed that Red wasn't as scruffy as he had at first thought. He also noticed that whilst one of his eyes was dark brown, the other was as blue as a summer sky.

Mr Wizard opened the door and Red obediently jumped into the back and settled himself in a coil. The seats were made of grey leather, not at all the sort of car that Mitch imagined Mr Wizard owning; up until that moment, Mr Wizard hadn't seemed like the "owning" sort.

Seeing that Mr Wizard had a very smart car didn't make Mitch feel any better, and what happened next made him feel a whole lot worse.

Mr Wizard took off the smelly coat and threw it into the bushes. Next, he eased his fingers under his hair-line and with a sharp tug pulled the matted curls clean off his head.

Mitch stared.

Without his hair and coat, Mr Wizard was utterly transformed.

The car was a bit stuffy. Mitch looked at the window and wondered if he could open it. There wasn't anything obvious as far as he could see. He also noticed that there was nothing that looked like a handle with which to open the door either, even if he was brave enough to jump out of a speeding car. He remembered the rolls they'd been doing in PE; all very well on a rubber mat but at 40 miles per hour? He looked out at the countryside, now lit only by the car's headlights.

He had absolutely no idea where they were.

The car radio was tuned to a news channel. There was a report about a bombing—somewhere foreign. Israel? Iraq? The reporter was interviewing a man who had lost his son. He was sobbing, screaming, and calling for revenge.

Mitch wondered if his dad would scream like that. *He probably wouldn't*, he thought. Probably, he'd be glad to get him off his hands, probably rent his bedroom to holiday-makers. A hot tear slipped down his cheek.

This was bad. He was in a car with a man who had pretended to be some kind of smelly low-life; even the dog had pretended to be some kind of smelly low-life, and he was being taken to, well, who knew where?

'Where are we going?' asked Mitch in a voice a little wobblier than usual.

'You'll see,' said the man who, it turned out, had very little hair at all and without the smelly coat looked like a don't-mess-with-me headmaster. Mitch had trouble remembering that just thirty minutes before he'd looked like a friendly tramp who had wanted to help.

'Is it far?'

'Nearly there as a matter of fact old son,' said the man, who might or might not have been called Mr Wizard.

The car turned down a gravel drive and stopped. There were no lights.

'Is this it?' asked Mitch. He glanced surreptitiously into the side mirror wondering if he could run back up the drive. As he looked, a tall iron gate slid across the entrance and blocked off the road. Before the lights from the car dimmed, he noticed that there was a coil of barbed wire threaded along the top.

'This,' said the man, 'is very much it.'

He got out of the car and reached inside for Mitch.

'No time to muck about sunshine,' he said, holding Mitch's arm and guiding him forcibly towards the front of a shuttered house. He pulled out a bunch of keys and unlocked a door. A smell of damp and dust hung around a dark hallway. Nobody appeared to be in.

'Get inside,' said the phoney wizard, pushing Mitch in front of him and pulling the door to with his foot. He double locked and bolted it, pocketed the keys and felt along the wall for a switch.

'No place like home eh son?' he said without the trace of a smile.

He went upstairs leaving Mitch alone in the gloomy hall.

He had no idea what the time was but it had to be really late. He wondered if he could phone home.

There was a phone mounted on the wall, the sort with a curly cord. Mitch could just about reach it. He picked up the receiver. It was dead.

'No use I'm afraid, old chap,' said the man suddenly reappearing. 'Cut-off. Like this house. Not a soul for miles and miles. Hungry?'

There was a rather dusty kitchen which smelt of stale milk.

The man opened the fridge and pulled out a bulging plastic bag full of wrapped sandwiches, which he shook out onto a table.

'There's Turkey and Cole Slaw, BLT, Ham and Mustard or,' he peered at the label on the last packet, 'oh dear! Roasted Vegetables! Nasty.'

'Excuse me,' said Mitch. 'I mean it's nice of you to take care of me and that, and I'm grateful, of course, and when my brother and my dad hear how kind you've been, they'll probably give you a reward or some such, but can we let them know where I am? I mean they'll get mad at me I expect to start with, but they might be worried. I mean to say it's dark. It's most probably my bed-time. Past my bed-time I should think.'

He stopped.

The bald-headed man was looking like someone whose patience was beginning to run out.

'You're very good I'll give you that, almost had me convinced there for a moment, but I think that's enough play acting for one evening don't you Jackson? It's been a very long day.'

Chapter Five

By the time they got to the police station it was late. Nate was shown into a room with computers and white boards, desks and plastic moulded seats. It felt a bit like school.

A woman stepped forward and held out her hand. 'Nathan Jackson? Your brother is the missing boy right? Mitchel Jackson?'

'We call him Mitch,' said Nate miserably.

The woman shook his hand and nodded kindly.

'I'm your liaison officer. Call me Carol. We're all working together on this one, Nathan. The first 24 hours are vital so we'll need as much information as possible. I'm going to be with you every step of the way.'

She ushered him to a seat and pushed a mug of tea towards him.

'We're trying to get hold of your parents, but in the meantime, I'll need a full description.'

Nate suddenly remembered something.

'There's this,' he said. He pulled out Dad's phone and scrawled through the options looking for photos.

'I took a load of photos at Nan's. She shaved his head, see? Mitch was dead chuffed.'

He showed Carol. She passed the phone to PC Lee who raised his eyebrows.

'No accounting for taste,' he said under his breath. 'I'll take a copy of this.'

Sanders looked across at PC Lee.

'Might even make the 10 o'clock news do you reckon John? South Today slot?'

Nate felt as though he'd been hit. The 10 o'clock news? He watched the news and read the papers; this was serious then. He remembered all the missing kids he'd ever heard about; snatched out of their beds or enticed away from their friends with the lure of a treat. He couldn't stop his imagination flooding his brain with horrible images of Mitch tied and gagged in the boot of a car, or beaten up and abandoned on a windswept moor, or even half-way across the Atlantic in a shipping container in the dark with no food or water.

'But, but—' he stammered, 'surely all you need to do is just check through the CCTV footage? He can't be far away can he? You said it was just an incident, not a full-scale thingy, not a what-do-you-call-it, abduction thingy.'

'Better be safe than sorry, son.'

'You reckon he's been murdered, don't you? He's only ten. I was supposed to look after him.'

Nate sunk his head onto his chest and used his forearm to wipe the tears off his cheek.

'I should have taken him to the toilet but I never realised, never thought. It's all my fault.' He looked up at the policemen and said again in a shaky voice, 'It's all my fault.'

Carol patted Nate's arm.

'You're doing fine,' she said. 'It would be really good if you could help us with the CCTV footage though. Do you reckon you can? Just while we wait for your parents?'

''Course. I'll do anything. Whatever you want.'

Nate, Sanders and Carol watched over John Lee's shoulder as he scrolled through jerky black and white shapes moving fuzzily across the screen.

'No point in going past 15:30 is there?' said Carol. 'Go back and have another look, both exits remember.'

PC Lee pressed a key, which reversed the tape and made the passengers jump backwards onto the train in a way that would have been funny if it wasn't so serious.

'Wait!' said Nate. 'Let me see that bit again.'

In the corner of the screen, only just visible, was the back of a small shaved head.

'That's him.' said Nate. 'Look! He's watching the passengers leave the station, watching what they do with their tickets. He wouldn't know what to do with his ticket because it's the first time Dad's let us do this on our own. It's the first time and I,' Nate gulped, 'I messed up.'

Carol touched his arm.

'Do you want a break?' she asked. 'Your dad should get here soon enough, soon as we can contact him. It is your *dad* you want us to contact and not your mum?'

'Yeah,' Nate gave an empty laugh. 'Well, if you contact my mum, tell her we're doing fine and thanks for asking...not!'

'I see.' Carol and Sanders exchanged looks over Nate's head. 'She doesn't live with you then?'

Nate shook his head wearily. He wasn't in the mood to talk about Mum.

'Right. The local Isle of Wight police are looking for your dad right now. He's not at home though. It was South Street? Number 12? Ventnor?'

Carol waited for Nate to answer. 'Nate? Have we got that right?'

Nate wasn't listening. He'd just realised something else.

'Dad's not picking up the phone at home because he's not in, like I said. He'll be waiting at the ferry terminal by now to pick us up. He probably went straight there from fishing. He hasn't got a mobile. He gave it to me don't you see? He'll be going mental.'

'We'll get in touch with your dad somehow Nate. Don't worry about that. We're more concerned about you and your brother.'

'I'm alright,' Nate said. 'I just want to find Mitch, that's all.'

'Aha! This might be handy.'

PC Lee had been staring at his screen and everyone crowded around.

'This is from the corner of the high street, where that cyclist got hit this afternoon remember? We had to divert everyone round the ring road? Look at this.'

On the screen was a boy, running backwards through the traffic and away from the snarl up, his hands in the air.

'Is that him?'

Everyone in the office looked at Nate.

'That's Mitch! There he is! That's him!' Nate almost shouted. He got closer to the screen and tried to touch him, pull him out of the TV screen.

'But look at the way he's running, and his face! I'd say he was scared, and when he runs, he gets asthma so he'll need his inhaler, and he hasn't got it.' Nate pointed miserably to the floor. 'It's here. In his bag.'

'Can you freeze that picture right there for a moment?' Carol was staring at the screen.

'That's weird,' she said. 'Look there.'

She pointed to the crowded pavement where people were craning their necks to see what was going on; a row of faces with one exception—a man with his back to the camera about to walk away, seemingly in a hurry.

'What's odd about that?' asked Sanders. 'Looks like a decent person wanting to keep his beak out, not poking around in other people's misery. Give him a sticker!'

'Yes, but can you zoom in on him, make him clearer?'

The man in a hurry, frozen mid-step, grew bigger.

'Nate, what can you see?' said Carol.

Nate peered closer to the screen.

'Looks like a bloke in a leather jacket.'

'Can we go closer?' asked Carol.

PC Lee expanded the image and the man grew larger and blurrier.

'Wait!' Nate stabbed his finger at the screen.

'Look! He's got a jacket just like mine!'

Everyone looked at Nate's jacket. It was made of leather, cracked and worn. "Vintage" Nan had called it. It was the sort of jacket that bikers wore. On the back was a printed picture of a wolf, its jaws wide open, and head lifted to a moon just rising behind a mountain peak. It wasn't an everyday sort of jacket.

'Planning on doing a ton up the motorway?' joked DI Sanders.

'Bit of a coincidence, wouldn't you say?' said Carol. 'I mean, you don't see a jacket like that for years and then two turn up. I don't like it.'

'What do you mean you don't like it?' said Nate indignantly. 'I've only just been given it. It was a present from Nan.'

'No, I don't mean I don't like your *jacket*,' said Carol, 'although to be honest, it's not really my cup of tea.' She looked at the screen again. 'No, what I don't like is coincidences. Something's not right here and my hunch tells me the answer's right in front of our noses.'

***

All the time Nate was in the police station and Mitch was who-knew-where, another boy sat alone on a bench in the car park of The Three Bells pub. He was skinny and pale. His mouth was open to help him breathe because his nose was blocked. It usually was. His eyes were sore from rubbing. His head felt cold. He shaved it himself whenever he had any money for razors. If anyone cared to look a little closer, they might make out the tip of a tattooed dagger pointing towards his neck from beneath his ragged T-shirt. Across the dagger was the boy's name pricked out in blue. "Jackson".

Chapter Six

Mitch couldn't sleep. His eyelids flickered every time he closed them, and his chest was getting tighter again. He would be all right if he could just sleep.

This time last night he was tucked up at Nan's on the sofa, tummy stuffed full of bangers and mash, snuggled down watching the Simpsons. Not a care. Not a clue. And now, because he had needed a wee, look at the mess he was in. He needed a wee again, he suddenly realised; probably wasn't helping, needing a wee, so better think of something else.

The man had said what exactly? Mitch tried to remember.

I think that's enough play-acting for one evening

Play-acting? What was that supposed to mean? Like being in a play? More like a horror movie…this was way scarier than anything he and Nate had ever seen, and the more he thought about it the scarier it felt and the more desperate he was for a wee. *Don't think about it. Think about the man.* He had said something else.

Mitch sat up with a jolt and banged his head as if trying to knock in some sense.

I think that's enough play-acting for one evening, JACKSON.

'He said *Jackson.* That's me. How did he know my name?'

Mitch was talking out loud. He wondered if he was going a bit bonkers, talking to no one. No surprise if he *was* going a bit barmy with the mess he was in. He gave himself a shake.

There wasn't a light in the room but he could see a crack under the door.

He got out of bed and tiptoed his way towards it. The door wasn't locked. That felt good for a moment, until he remembered the sliding iron gate and the barbed wire.

On the landing, he could see the bathroom across the landing. He also heard Mr Wizard answering his mobile.

'Hello? Yes, of course, it's me…I'm at the house…with our small friend, yes.'

A whimper from behind Mitch made him jump. Red!

'Hang on, old chap…there's someone moving around…I'll ring you back.'

Mitch forgot all about wanting a wee and skidded back into bed, pulling up the itchy blanket, and shutting his eyes.

The door opened and footsteps tiptoed across the floor towards him. He fought the pain in his chest and tried to breathe regularly as if he was asleep. He felt the man staring down at him. It seemed like ages. Then he tiptoed back out only this time there was the sound of metal being turned in the lock.

The night went on forever. He tried every trick he knew to get off to sleep such as reciting the names of the children in his class or making every muscle in his body from his toes to his head clench and relax. He counted backwards in twos from one thousand. Nothing worked. His eyes were grainy and raw, his head ached more than ever. He knew if he didn't get to sleep soon, he'd see the telly in his head playing a sequence of pictures he tried to forget. Pictures of him and Mum up on the downs, him and Mum eating ice cream on the beach, Mum running into the surf dressed as a Christmas fairy for the Boxing Day Swim. No, he couldn't watch those pictures now, not when his inhaler was miles and miles away.

There were shutters across the window, fastened from the outside, but they let in a slim crack of light, which grew brighter with the morning. He heard a bird start to call and then another and another until the sound filled the room. He hadn't ever noticed things like birds before, not really. He didn't have a clue what they were called either. Well, perhaps pigeons and maybe robins off Christmas cards. He made up his mind to learn all about them—all about their songs, what they ate, where they lived. Not take them for granted, actually not take anything for granted if he could just get out of this mess.

Chapter Seven

'Nate?' Carol was shaking him by the shoulder. He must have dropped off. It took him a while to work out where he was.

'What's the time?' He rubbed his hands across his face as if he was washing with water.

'Two a.m. Your dad rang. He saw the news I'm afraid, before we got to him. Must have been a shock.'

'Yeah, him and me both.'

Nate wondered if Mitch had seen the news too from wherever he was. Maybe a kidnapper was even now preparing a ransom letter. Nate snorted at the thought: fat chance of raising a laugh, never mind a ransom.

Seeing Mitch on the telly had been surreal. The photo with that haircut Nan had done made Mitch look like he'd deserved to get lost somehow, like he was a little toughie who'd run away on purpose; made him look older than he really was.

Carol put another mug of tea down on the table.

'I'm sorry to keep on at you Nate it's just, well we need a few more details, about the weekend? It might help us find him.'

Nate looked gloomily into his tea.

'I've told you everything already.'

'Possibly, yes.' Carol got out her notebook. 'Where were you staying again?'

'Nan's. Never been up on our own before.'

'And where does she live?'

'London.'

'It's a big place, London.'

Nate shrugged.

'I dunno the address. I mean we never write to each other. She phones.'

He thought again.

'I know what it looks like, I mean I'd recognize it.'

'Well, what happened when you got to Waterloo? It was Waterloo I take it, not Victoria?'

Nate nodded, 'She met us, and we got a bus. We went through loads of streets and that. Her flat is by a park.'

'Well that should narrow it down a bit,' muttered PC Lee.

'OK, we'll get back to that.'

Carol let Nate take a moment as she looked at her notes.

'Your mum,' said Carol.

'What about her?'

'How come you don't know where she is?'

Nate shook his head but Carol persisted. 'I'm sorry to ask this, I can see it's painful, but what happened exactly?'

'How's this going to help? We're wasting time here.'

Carol patted his arm.

'As I said, the more information we have, the better.'

Nate sighed. He'd told this over and over again, mainly at school. His mates were dead jealous; no mum nagging at you, making you do stuff. They had no idea how hard it was especially with Dad so low.

'She left us OK?'

Carol nodded. 'Yes, you said. When?'

'It was Friday, the week after she opened her new premises, almost two months ago now.'

'What premises?' asked Carol.

'Mum's new salon. It's called Head Hunter. That was my idea matter of fact.' Nate allowed himself a modest smile.

'She's a hairdresser, a good one and all; that is she *was*.' Nate bit his lip. 'She got to be so popular she had to open a bigger place and get an assistant. All the ladies in Ventnor went to Mum's. They all liked her, even the old crusties did.'

'What happened to the new shop after she left?'

'It shut, of course. It's just as she left it though. Dad paid a year's rent up front. That's what we couldn't understand. She'd been so excited about Head Hunter, had it all decorated and kitted out. We had an opening party and the County Press came and everything. Mum's photo was on the front page.'

'Go on then,' said Carol. 'What happened next?'

'She went into the shop early, said she had a customer, so we three—me and Mitch and Mum, we all walked down to the town together. The school bus stops just over the way from the shop see.'

Nate looked away from Carol.

She said, 'Love you guys.' She gave us a hug.

Nate didn't notice his tears this time. He didn't care.

'Then what?' said Carol gently.

'The bus came,' said Nate. 'It came and I didn't want Mum hugging us. There was a load of kids all trying to get to the back of the bus. The heel on my trainer got trodden on and it nearly came off, so I had to push my foot back in. I was left on the pavement for a minute.'

Nate paused. He looked at the policemen.

'I saw something weird then. I looked over to the shop and Mum's customer, her "early", was a bloke.'

'What was weird about that?' asked Carol.

'She never did blokes. There's a barber's as well in Ventnor. He does the blokes.'

'A bloke? What sort of bloke?' said Carol.

'I don't know. I couldn't really see. Just a bloke.'

She paused for Nate to continue and when he didn't, she asked, 'Did your mum and dad get on? Had there been any arguments?'

'That's the thing, Mitch and I always thought they did. But they couldn't have could they else why did she go? Unless, maybe she was just fed up with being a mum.'

Carol put her hand on Nate's, but he hardly noticed.

'Dad's gone mental looking for her. He went to the police. He gave them a really good description, and a photo of her with him, and us. They asked if she'd taken anything important, like a passport or anything. He said we haven't got passports…never needed them see, but the awful thing was what happened when Dad got back.'

'Go on,' said Carol.

'Dad came back to the house from the station. He stood in the kitchen and he stared at the fridge.'

'Why?'

He stared at the fridge and then he said to us, 'She's gone. She's gone on purpose. Look.'

'The fridge had those plastic magnetic letters. We used to make words with them when we were little only now we don't use them for that, just for magnets. Well she'd put Mitch's school photo on with the M and mine was stuck on with the N. And they weren't there. Dad said, "She's gone and she's taken those photos." So then we knew see? She hadn't just got lost or wandered off. She'd planned to go.'

Nate tried not to cry again but he couldn't help it.

'The police, they said that she most probably done a runner, probably gone off with a bloke they said. They said if they got involved every time someone's wife walked out there'd be no time for nothing else.'

'Did you tell the police what you saw?'

Nate shook his head.

'I never did because they never asked and I never told Dad because he was so upset and I thought it would make him feel worse, knowing there was this bloke I saw with Mum.'

'You've had a rough time,' said Carol.

'It's OK,' said Nate. 'We get on with it—me and Mitch and Dad. But this, this thing with Mitch...' he shook his head, 'I dunno how he'll hack it.'

DI Sanders cleared his throat. 'I'm sorry for you lad,' he said 'but the clock's ticking. Can we get back to the jacket? Where did it come from?'

'I dunno,' said Nate. 'I've only just got it this weekend.'

'Got it from where?'

'We got it off Nan. She said we could keep it. I and Mitch found it at the back of the garden shed.'

'Doesn't look like the sort of jacket your average granny might buy. What is she? A Hells Angel or Hell's Granny or whatever?' PC Lee chuckled at his little joke.

'It wasn't hers,' said Nate. 'Nan just said if we wanted it she supposed it would be alright after all this time for us to have it.'

He chewed at his thumb.

'Trouble was there was only one and we both wanted it, Mitch and me. Mitch got really upset. He got himself in a state, nearly had an asthma attack. Well that made Nan worried, of course, and I was really cross with Mitch for being such a spoilt baby. It didn't fit him. You can see it would be too big for him and besides, he isn't old enough for a jacket like this.'

'Whereas, of course, you are?' asked PC Lee.

Carol frowned at him.

'Anyway, Nan said if Mitch let me have the jacket she'd give Mitch a special haircut with her special barber's scissors, only it went a bit wrong so Nan had to shave it all off. Mitch didn't mind. I told him he could have the jacket when he was bigger anyway.'

DI Sanders had been listening quietly.

'You said there was only one jacket. You were wrong about that. There are two. And the other one is being worn by whoever your brother followed off that train.'

Chapter Eight

The person Mitch had followed off the train was called Mr Wolf. It wasn't his real name, of course, but it certainly suited him.

He had a particularly long nose and rather pointed ears. His eyes were more yellow than was healthy. They remained dry, generally speaking. He was not a sentimental man, some might say far from it. The only time he had ever cried in his whole life was when his dog, Loopy, had got run over. He'd wrapped him up in a blanket and put him in a dustbin; saddest day of his life. He vowed never to get another dog but he looked out for them so to speak.

Walking about in London he never looked at faces, he looked at dogs, and they looked back. He could stare a dog down, get it to whine or yelp. He had a knack. It was something he thought he could always fall back on if the "courier" business got a bit, well, "complicated" should he say.

Yes, he knew his dogs alright which was how he'd taken so long to get to The Three Bells.

When he'd come out of the shop with his lottery ticket, there was a crowd of people staring at some accident. The road was blocked. He'd decided to walk a different way, follow his nose. He always kept away from crowds. As he'd walked, he'd heard a siren wailing closer, threading its way through the jam; all the more reason to go a different way.

He had just got to the corner of the street near the Shopping Centre when he'd seen the dog.

It was a German shepherd, nothing unusual in that, of course. One of the commonest breeds—an Alsatian—named after a region in France near the German border, Alsace; he remembered looking it up on Wikipedia when he was trying to work out what breed Loopy was. But this dog had a different tail from a true Alsatian, and more hair; like a police dog, *exactly like a police dog*, thought Mr Wolf. And another thing; one of his eyes was the usual brown whereas the other one was an ice-cold blue. The dog was lying on the pavement, its tongue lolling out, a scarf around its neck for a collar and a piece of string for a lead. The man who was with him was leaning casually against the wall, a pile of magazines at his feet, talking to someone on a mobile phone. He was wearing a filthy coat, which dragged, along the floor, and his hair hung in knotted spirals around his shoulders

The dog had looked at Mr Wolf and Mr Wolf had looked straight back, staring into the blue eye and the brown eye, expecting the dog to wag its tail, but the dog didn't; its hackles rippled along its spine and its upper lip curled into a snarl. It got into an alarming pounce position with its haunches raised.

Mr Wolf shrunk back into a doorway and made himself small. The tatty string didn't fool Mr Wolf; that was a well-nourished, healthy and highly trained dog; he could see his nose shining from here. So, what was he doing with a dosser? Come to think of it, what was the dosser doing with a mobile phone?

Mr Wolf had sucked his teeth and narrowed his eyes. Something was wrong, he could smell it. He had backed away as unobtrusively as possible before the dosser was attracted by the dog's growls, and as soon as he was far enough away he had turned and retraced his steps back to the shop where he'd bought his lottery ticket.

The police were now at the scene of the accident. Mr Wolf edged around the crowd with his head down. A van driver was shouting that it wasn't his fault, it was a boy, the one who had just run out in front of a cyclist.

Mr Wolf had hurried on towards The Three Bells. He had an urgent meeting with a new employee and he was late.

***

Jackson, the boy all alone in the pub car park with his tattooed neck, stood up and yawned.

He rubbed his hand over his head and down the first few vertebra of his spine. Although he couldn't feel it, he knew the tattooed tip of the dagger was there, a warning to others not to mess.

There was no one here except him. He must have got the wrong place. He shrugged his thin shoulders. Too bad. He'd been told to meet a bloke called Mr Wolf who would help him out, give him some money, set him right. He blamed the waste of space who'd given him the message in the first place, a bloke called Ferris. Whatever. Jackson was used to things not turning out so well. He didn't ever expect much and he was never disappointed. He was always hungry though and now he remembered he hadn't eaten since yesterday.

Someone had left a greasy paper from some chips on one of the pub tables. There was a bottle of ketchup too. Quickly, Jackson smeared ketchup over the greasy paper and licked it off. The smell of the chips only made him hungrier.

It was time to go.

Chapter Nine

Mitch sat at the kitchen table. It was Monday, a whole day after he'd gone for a wee on a train.

In another universe, on another planet, kids would be getting up, watching cartoons, eating cereal and toast. They'd be fighting with their brothers and sisters, dawdling in the bathroom, pulling faces in the mirror, ignoring the shouts of "hurry up".

Mitch's Monday wasn't like that, not now. On the table, there was a bar of chocolate and a packet of crisps. He loved stuff like that normally, but now just the thought of crisps made him feel queasy. His clothes smelled horrible and the inside of his mouth was furry.

'Fine dining, eh,' said Mr Wizard, ripping open a smoky bacon smelling packet and digging his hand inside. 'Eat up, Jackson. Then we can get down to business.'

'What business?' asked Mitch, 'I'll co-operate like you said. Honestly, it's just I don't know what I'm co-operating about.' Mitch felt on the verge of tears. 'Mr Wizard, sir,' he added.

Mr Wizard munched his way through another packet of crisps, balled up the bag and threw it into the corner of the room.

'How's the lump?' he asked suddenly, walking round the table to have a look.

Mitch put his hands up defensively.

'I'm not going to hurt you boy! Co-operation I said, not coercion.'

He walked behind Mitch.

'That's odd.' He pulled at the back of Mitch's sweater, tugging it against his throat.

'You're strangling me,' said Mitch.

'Take your sweater off. Now.'

Something in the man's voice had Mitch fumbling to take his sweater off as soon as possible.

'Where's the dagger?' asked Mr Wizard. 'What have you done with the dagger?'

'I don't know what you mean,' stammered Mitch. 'I haven't got a dagger.'

Mr Wizard stared at Mitch. He held him by his shoulders and looked into his face.

'Who exactly are you?'

'I'm Mitch,' said Mitch. 'Mitch Jackson. I thought you knew.'

Mr Wizard sat down heavily on one of the chairs.

'But you said you were a runaway, that you'd left your mum!'

'No I never! I said she left us. And I never ran away.'

'So that fairy story you told me in the bus shelter, all that stuff about getting off the train…'

'But it's true! I was following my brother like I said. Only, see, it wasn't my brother.'

'Why in the name of all that's holy did you think it was?'

'He was wearing Nate's jacket. I told you.'

'What made you so sure it was Nate's jacket? What was it, covered in diamonds and flashing lights?'

'Nah nothing like that. Nate's jacket's wicked though. It's got like, a wolf on the back?'

Mr Wizard's eyes narrowed.

'A wolf? Did you say a wolf? Howling at the moon against a rocky mountain landscape sort of thing?'

'Yes!' said Mitch. 'How did you know that?'

'Call it intuition.'

Mr Wizard got up and paced the floor.

'This jacket, where did your brother get it come from?'

'My Nan's. We found it in her shed. We both wanted to keep it but it fitted Nate really.' Mitch looked at his feet. 'I might have gone off on one, just a bit.'

Thinking back Mitch could hardly believe he'd made such a fuss; it had seemed the biggest deal ever that Nate got to keep the jacket and not him. He'd behaved like a three-year-old kid, he realised that now, and it wasn't until Nan promised to shave his head like he'd been wanting for ages that he'd begun to calm down.

'Nan said she'd shave my head to make it fair.'

'What do you mean, fair?'

'I was a bit, like you know, mad, that Nate got the jacket? I may have been a bit moody so Nan made it fair like I said, see?'

'If you say so,' said Mr Wizard looking doubtfully at Mitch's shorn head. 'At any rate, it's what you might call a close shave, in all senses of the word. If Nate hadn't found the jacket, your Nan wouldn't have shaved your head, and if you hadn't looked like an ex-con...some sort of ragamuffin...no offence, old son.'

Mr Wizard thought for a moment.

'You really did get off the train from London because you thought you saw your brother getting off too?'

Mitch nodded. 'Honest. I told you.'

'And you thought he was your brother because he was wearing an old leather jacket with a wolf on the back? Yes?'

'Yes,' said Mitch.

'And this jacket was the jacket your Nan had given your brother the day before? Am I OK so far?'

Mitch nodded again.

'And your Nan, where did she get the jacket from?'

'She never said.'

Mr Wizard looked hard at Mitch.

'Ever heard of a chap named Ferris?'

'Ferris? Never.' Mitch shook his head.

'And you weren't expecting to meet anyone at The Three Bells pub?'

'I don't know any Three Bells Pub. I was just looking for Nate.'

'That settles it,' said Mr Wizard. 'No good beating about the bush, young Mitch. There's been a mix-up; a right old Horlicks of a mix-up.'

He looked to Red for confirmation.

'I know we haven't exactly got off to a brilliant start; I may have been a little, well, forceful?'

Mitch wondered what he was going to say next.

He wouldn't have guessed in a million years.

'If,' said Mr Wizard, holding up a warning finger as if to emphasise the condition of his offer, 'you are prepared to be my, what shall we say, accomplice, I may, just may, have the power to grant your dearest wish.'

'How do you know what my dearest wish is?' asked Mitch suspiciously.

Mr Wizard came closer and whispered everything that Mitch could possibly hope for in one amazing sentence.

'Wow!' said Mitch. 'Can you really do that?'

'I can if you can. It'll mean you keeping this,' he pointed to Mitch's mouth, 'zipped. You savvy?'

'I'm really good at zipping. Honest!'

'In which case, I'll do everything in my power to make your dreams come true, you can trust me on that at least, *partner!*'

It took an hour to get to the police station. Red hung over the car seat and pressed his nose against Mitch's neck. Mitch didn't mind. He was numb with relief, delighted that this terrible nightmare might be ending.

He took deep breaths of fresh air out of the car window, his lungs allowing oxygen all the way in without a single wheeze. In his lap was the wrapper from a stale roasted vegetable sandwich, the most delicious meal he had ever eaten.

Mr Wizard had said he could make his dearest wish come true and now that they were partners, why, anything was possible.

'What are those birds called Mr Wizard, the ones on the telegraph line?'

'Starlings,' said the man, 'and by the way, the name's not Wizard. You must have heard wrong. It's Ezard.'

Chapter Ten

The three Jacksons—Dad, Nate and Mitch—were on all the news bulletins that evening and in all the papers the next day. The one Mitch liked best was the picture of him and Red, under the caption:

Nick Nack! Mitch Is Back! Give The Dog A Bone!

Missing 10-year-old Mitch Jackson was back with his family in Ventnor on the Isle of Wight last night, none the worse for his adventure. Mitch and his brother Nate had been travelling back to the Island when Mitch unexpectedly disappeared from the train.

'I thought I saw my brother get off,' said Mitch, 'so I got off too.'

An extensive search went on throughout the night involving police forces from two counties, but it was sharp-nosed Red who saved the day.

'He saved my life!' said Mitch who was found semi-conscious under a tree near the Hogs Back at 7:00 this morning. Red the Alsatian and his owner, who prefers to remain anonymous, were taking their usual morning walk when Red started sniffing and licking something lying on the ground. 'It was the best early morning wash I've ever had!' grinned Mitch, who couldn't remember how he came to have passed out. Doctors who examined young Mitch concluded that the bump he got on his head could have caused temporary amnesia.

'*I'm just glad to have my boys back,*' *said single father of two, Joe Jackson. 'And I'll be thinking twice before I let either of them on a train again.*'

'See?' said Nate. 'Thanks to your bladder we probably won't ever be able to leave the Island again!'

'You don't want to believe everything you read in the papers mate,' said Mitch.

***

The Press Conference had been particularly trying; Detective Inspector Sanders hated loose ends and this case had more ends than a packet of spaghetti.

'I'm not happy,' said DI Sanders to Mr Ezard after the last of the reporters had been sent away. 'A happy bunny I am not.'

'Your emotional state is not my problem old man. As I explained, this is all strictly hush-hush. You blow my undercover operation and thirteen months of hard graft goes down the pan. We were this close last night.' He held his finger just above his thumb to indicate a very small amount of space. 'I thought for a moment we'd cracked it, but I'm not giving up, not at all. I'll catch the wicked wolf, don't you worry about that.'

DI Sanders and Carol exchanged glances.

'Did I say wolf? Figure of speech.' Mr Ezard looked at his watch. 'Right! Well! Can't hang about here. I need to get back to HQ; I've got a few enquiries to make. Watch this space, old chap, watch this space!'

Giving DI Sanders a half wave, half salute, he picked up his coat and left.

Carol put down two mugs of tea.

'Good riddance if you ask me,' she said. 'I hate those spooks and their under-cover carry on. And what was all that about a wolf?'

DI Sanders stared out of the window at the car park. Mr Ezard was getting into a very posh car. He saw there was a dog in the back seat.

'Looks like a wolf he's got in the back of his car.'

Carol joined him at the window.

'Do you believe what the lad Mitch said? All that stuff about getting concussion and not remembering what happened?'

'I'll believe in the tooth fairy first,' snorted Sanders. 'I doubt we'll ever get to the bottom of it all, but at least the boy's been found, and not by any wolf!'

Chapter Eleven

Mr Wolf lived quietly alone in a flat on Wolverton Drive, Hackney; it suited him very well. First, it was below ground level; he didn't like the sun. Next, it had its own entrance and no access for nosy neighbours. He'd put bars on the windows and across the door, just in case anyone got any ideas.

Best of all it had three dark storage rooms hidden at the back.

You wouldn't know they were there, not from the outside; nor from the inside come to that. He'd pushed a wardrobe across the only entrance. Those storage rooms were better than lock-ups or safes. He had all kinds of packages hidden in there, oh yes; packages for sale, packages for delivery, small ones, heavy ones, light ones, big ones, and pretty soon, of course, *breathing* ones.

It was what Mr Wolf did. He delivered and collected things that couldn't go in the post: things that needed to be hidden; things that might not be strictly legal; things that, should they ever be found by the wrong people, could get him into big trouble.

Mr Wolf had got back to his flat, some might even call it a lair, very late and cross. The day had been a waste of his time, and he felt more relieved than usual to bolt and bar the front door, pull off his jacket and flop down on a fur-covered sofa with his feet on the table. He put his hands behind his head and thought hard, trying to put his finger on what had gone wrong.

He'd got the train no trouble and got off at the right station. He'd got his lottery ticket at a shop near the station. But then, then there was the accident.

That accident had been the start of it because he'd taken a different route to the Three Bells and seen that dog.

He felt himself getting agitated at the thought of the dog with the mean blue eye. The dog had made him late so that when he got to the pub the boy he was going to meet, Jay? Jason? No *Jackson,* that was it, was nowhere to be seen. That was a nuisance that was. By the sound of it, Jackson was just the sort of boy he needed for his new venture, if indeed he even existed. It was Ferris who'd arranged the meeting...Ferris's fault then. Ferris better watch out. He was getting to be a liability.

Mr Wolf sighed. Business was booming and he needed younger staff, someone he could train to act as bait, someone who would attract other boys and girls.

He went into the kitchen and looked in the fridge. Food was what he needed, he couldn't think on an empty stomach. He made himself a triple-decker bacon sandwich and slunk back to the sitting room. He settled himself down on the furry sofa and stared moodily around him.

Mr Wolf had a vast collection of wolves; wolves on mugs, plates, posters and cushions. The flat was stuffed with them. It was surprising where and on what they turned up. He'd got ornaments made from china and glass, wolf motifs on shirts and sweaters, even one painted on his jacket.

Whilst he was eating his sandwich he flicked on the TV.

Some kid was missing; the boy's dad and a policeman were asking for witnesses. Mr Wolf took a professional interest in missing kids especially as this one was just where he'd been that very same day. He turned up the volume. Now they were interviewing the boy's brother.

Mr Wolf froze, his sandwich half-way to his mouth, the boy was wearing *his* jacket.

He stared at Nate. A piece of bacon fell from his open and astonished mouth onto his lap.

'This does not smell right, Wolfy,' he said out loud. 'Not right at all.'

Next morning, Mr Wolf was still on the fur-covered sofa, an empty plate with smears of bacon fat on the floor beside him. He had eventually dropped off, still fretting over the events of the day and wondering what the connection was to the boy in the jacket, for he was sure that there were connections to be made.

His neck ached from sleeping at an awkward angle.

The TV was still on. Breakfast News. They'd found the missing boy.

There was a picture of the same boy from last night's news, still wearing the jacket, and a bloke who looked like the boy's father, They were both hugging some little urchin with a shaved head.

'How sweet,' sneered Mr Wolf.

The reporter turned to the camera to say that a man walking his dog had found the missing boy under a tree. The man wanted to remain anonymous but his dog should get the credit.

There was the little kid being licked all over by a dog.

Mr Wolf jumped off the sofa and grabbed the controls. He pressed the live pause button. The image on the screen froze as the dog faced the camera, its one blue and one brown eye staring straight into Mr Wolf's flat.

'The DOG! *The* DOG! That's the DOG.'

'This is beginning to really stink,' said Mr Wolf, his voice getting louder, and if anyone had been listening they might almost have thought that he wasn't so much shouting as howling.

Chapter Twelve

The boy called Jackson—the boy that Mr Wolf had failed to meet—lived by himself on a strip of wasteland just below the busy main road from Guildford to Portsmouth, in a caravan.

The caravan had been abandoned on the wasteland, even though there was a notice that said "No Tipping". The notice was more of an invitation than a warning; there were at least three rusting cars, fridges and freezers, several sofas and a bedstead as well as a small mountain of black plastic bags. Since the council had opened an official municipal recycling centre some miles away however, Jackson had the site more or less to himself.

He'd been in the van at least a year, or so he thought. He could tell the time, it was a knack he had, but he'd begun to lose track of the months, it didn't seem important. It wasn't like he needed to remember much. He thought he was probably 15 now anyway because his birthday had always been about the same time as his eyes and nose started to stream and itch with hay fever. He'd been sneezing for a while.

He was proud of that van. He kept it nice.

The hardest thing to sort had been the water because, of course, there wasn't any.

When he'd first moved in, after the bust-up with his mum and her loser boyfriend Gary, he was amazed at how much he missed turning on the tap. He had never been that bothered about washing, but he hated the stink of the dossers and drop-outs he knew. Dossers like Ferris. He didn't want to stink like them but it was hard without water. Making a drink, having a dump, it was all a bit problematic. In the end, he'd dug a deep hole as far from the van as he could, like in the army. He'd seen a program about it on the telly so he knew that's what they did. He'd even got a plank so that he could sit with his bum over the pit. It wasn't too bad. He'd got used to it.

He'd collected containers and put them all around the van for catching rainwater, and at night he took an empty plastic bottle to the Service Station and filled up from the outside tap. It tasted alright. They chucked out food too. He just hung about and waited for the manager to lock up and leave the bins out. Usually, it was sandwiches but sometimes there were pies or sausage rolls, he wasn't fussy.

No, the van was alright, *he* was alright, except he was broke, which was how come he'd been waiting all flipping afternoon for this Mr Wolf character. Ferris, the rat, had assured him he was just right for the job—said this Mr Wolf was looking for a lad just like him, that he was ideal for what Mr Wolf had in mind. Not that Jackson had a single clue what was in this bloke's mind, nor Ferris' come to that, even supposing he had a mind, which was unlikely with all the cider Ferris drank. Jackson hated drunks. His mum's loser boyfriend was a drunk.

After he'd waited at The Three Bells, he'd tried the Three Bishops, then The Bellingham and finally he'd gone back to The Three Bells, but there was nothing and no one. Maybe Ferris was stringing him along.

Jackson kept the caravan padlocked, and he carried the key round his neck. He was surprised, then angry—to see that the lock had been broken and that the door was hanging open. Heavy smoke from a cigarette wafted through the gap. Jackson hated smoke. It made his eyes sting worse than ever. He picked up a broken bottle lying in the grass and tiptoed towards the window at the lounge end of the van. Lying across the window seat with his filthy feet up on the cushions was Ferris looking as if he owned the place.

Jackson burst in.

'Oi, who said you could make yourself at home?' he demanded as Ferris rolled off the narrow bench and onto the floor in shock.

'Streuth!' said Ferris, clutching at his heart. He stared at Jackson with his bloodshot eyes. 'Jackson!'

'Who were you expecting? The Easter Bunny?' said Jackson pushing Ferris back onto the floor, 'Don't you know it's rude to go visiting without an invitation?'

Jackson jabbed at Ferris' shoulder, each jab harder than the one before.

'I asked you a question, what's going on?'

'Easy, son,' said Ferris, 'I didn't think you'd be coming back so soon. You don't begrudge a poor old man a bit of a rest now do you?'

'Give over Ferris. This is my van. You're trespassing you are, and you stink.'

Jackson was slight but he was strong. He heaved Ferris up by his grubby lapels, keeping his face away from the old man's foul breath and tried to push him towards the door. He could see greasy lines of dirt in the crevices around Ferris' neck, and long grey hairs growing out of his ears.

'You're a capital L Loser do you know that?'

He let go of Ferris who lost his balance and crumpled into a heap on the ground.

'I said I'm sorry Jackson. I'll make it up to you honest. Get you another padlock if that's what you're worried about.'

Jackson remembered something. 'What did you mean, just then, when you said you didn't think I'd be coming back so soon?'

'I thought, well, wasn't you meeting up with Mr Wolf today?' Ferris lifted himself a little way off the floor and gave Jackson a sly glance.

'What if I was?' said Jackson.

'Well did you see him then? Did he give you a job?' Ferris' ferrety eyes shot another sneaky look at Jackson, as if he was trying to read something in his face.

'No, because, you disgusting old perv, you sent me on a wild goose chase, didn't you? He was never going to show, was he? This was a set up to get into my caravan and have a doss, wasn't it?'

For once, Ferris looked a little more relaxed.

'On my mother's life, I swear, Jackson, I never. Mr Wolf wanted to meet up with you for sure.'

'Whatever,' said Jackson, suddenly tired and wanting Ferris out of the caravan and far away, 'just go! Go, before I need a bleeding oxygen mask.'

After Ferris had left, he opened the door as wide as he could to let out the smell.

Under a blanket, he found three bottles of cider and a family-sized fried chicken waxed bucket, all empty, which was odd; not because they were empty but because normally Ferris had barely enough money for a packet of salted crisps.

Chapter Thirteen

It took a day and a night for Ferris to get back up to London. He got a lift as far as Croydon sitting in the back of a truck, then he walked a long way with his eyes on the ground before he saw a card dropped in the gutter. It was an Oyster card which he could use as a ticket on buses and trains as long as it still had credit.

He took the bus to Hackney and managed to have a little kip; sleep and eat whenever you can—first rule of the street. The eating part was harder, and he needed a drink.

He couldn't focus very well, his head ached, and his mouth was dry.

Mr Wolf's flat was shuttered and barred but Ferris rang the bell all the same. He heard someone come to the door and take a while to unfasten the bolts.

'Streuth,' said Ferris when Mr Wolf finally opened the door. 'What big bolts you got.'

'All the better to keep you out,' muttered Mr Wolf, 'but as you're here you may as well come in. Besides, I've got a bone to pick with you.'

Ferris sat down on the fur-covered sofa.

'Get your filthy coat off my skins,' growled Mr Wolf.

Ferris jumped up and stood awkwardly by the door.

'Your boy, Jackson? The one you said would be a good worker? He never showed, Ferris, and now I'm wondering what your little game is.'

'He was there alright Mr W,' said Ferris using the wheedling voice he saved for moments such as this. 'He was, honest! He waited at the Three Bells like we agreed and then when you didn't show…'

Mr Wolf snarled. 'Didn't show? I showed alright. Got myself all tangled up in some accident and then had a very close encounter with the law.'

'What?' Ferris looked genuinely surprised.

'Oh he wasn't "uniform" but he didn't fool me, not for a moment. He was in some sort of disguise, and he was waiting and watching, not far from the pub. He had a dog.'

Ferris felt a bit faint.

'How did you know he was the law?'

'I've got a nose for it Ferris, I notice things other people don't bother with, see? Trust me, it was the law.'

Mr Wolf looked at Ferris sharply.

'You don't know anything about this man and his dog do you?'

'Dog? No way! I don't know no dogs Mr W. Dog? 'Course not. I'm more of a cat man.'

'Only if I thought you'd set me up...'

'Set you up, Mr W? What on earth makes you think that?'

Mr Wolf gave Ferris a long hard stare before he continued.

'Anyway he didn't show and I wasn't going to hang about. I hate being in the country. All that...' Mr Wolf considered what it was he hated about the country, 'all that *"outside"*. Nowhere to be private like.'

Mr Wolf flipped off the lid of a bottle of beer with his teeth. Ferris eyed it longingly but knew better than to ask.

'I suppose you know I've got a customer waiting?' said Mr Wolf. 'That boy Jackson was just the sort of lad to help attract the kind of thing my customer wants. Bait you might say.'

Mr Wolf swigged back his beer and belched loudly. He pointed at Ferris with a long finger nail.

'Can't be helped, Ferris. You'll have to do it instead,' he said.

Ferris gawped. 'Count me out Mr W. I mean I don't mind doing errands, taking messages, even looking for "opportunities", but I draw the line at taking...*livestock.*'

Mr Wolf leapt off the sofa and pushed Ferris painfully against the door.

'I don't remember offering you a choice,' he snarled. 'It's bad for business, letting clients down.'

He kept his arm pushed across Ferris's chest. Ferris noticed that he had hair on the back of his hand. Mr Wolf pushed harder until Ferris felt dizzy.

'No worries, Mr W,' Ferris gasped. 'Tell me what you want.'

Mr Wolf eased off a little allowing Ferris to catch his breath.

'Get me some fresh meat…soonest! Anything decent, but nothing too old. Get me?'

Ferris nodded bleakly.

'I should have stuck to *"inanimates"*,' Mr Wolf muttered. 'Much easier to handle if you get my drift. Still no pain no gain as my dear old ma used to say.'

Ferris wondered what Mr Wolf's dear old ma might have looked like; he had an unpleasant image in his mind of a wolf in bed, dressed in a nightgown and wearing a frilly cap, waiting for Red Riding Hood to call.

'Get on with it then, Ferris you skunk,' said Mr Wolf. 'Don't stand there stinking my nice flat out. You'll get your cash, don't worry about that.'

Ferris nodded and turned to go. He was just through the door when Mr Wolf called him back.

'Don't forget to use Roxy,' he said. 'You can rely on her at least.'

***

After Ferris left Wolverton Drive, he headed for London Bridge. It was late by the time he got there and the stalls were closing. He rummaged in a bin near the coffee shop.

The butcher from the Spicy Pig shouted over.

'Oi mate! There was a geezer here looking for you.'

'Oh yeah? How do you know it was me?'

'Your Gucci shoes, granddad! They're a dead giveaway.'

'Funny. You should go on the telly.' said Ferris. He rubbed his hands together and tried a smile. 'I don't suppose you've got any change to spare have you son?'

'Change?' The butcher screwed up his nose, 'You could do with a change mate. Go on then.'

He dug in his pocket and gave Ferris a two pound coin.

'Good on you,' said Ferris. 'This gentleman, the one what was looking for me, what did you say his name was?'

'I didn't,' said the butcher. 'He's in here regularly though; he gets bones for his dog. He'll be in tomorrow most like.'

A dog? Ferris sighed. A man with a dog, looking for him? That could only mean one person. Mr Ezard was looking for him and Mr Ezard was not to be ignored.

After the water cart had washed through the alleyways and the pubs and bars were finally closed, Ferris curled up by a hot air vent off the pavement and shut his eyes. The rats ignored him, looking for something more edible under the market stalls.

The first trains out of London Bridge rattled him awake and he sat himself up and stared groggily around him. He thought wistfully of Jackson's cosy caravan. There were times when a few mod cons wouldn't be unwelcome. The market was beginning to open up. Shutters were coming off stalls, delivery vans backing into the narrow passageways.

It was midday before he saw a familiar brown and black dog with one blue and one brown eye come sniffing around the corner and pause in front of him before barking and whining at his ankles.

'Ferris you villain,' said a cultured voice. 'What kept you? Stretch limousine in for a service?''

'Give me a break Mr E. I've been waiting since Monday.'

'You're a ruddy liar! He's a ruddy liar isn't he Red?'

Red snarled and allowed Ferris a glimpse of his perfectly sharpened side teeth.

'I don't know what you mean Mr E, honest I don't.' Ferris couldn't concentrate with those fangs so close to his leg.

'The words, *Ferris* and *honest*...' Mr Ezard looked sad. 'Not two words you *often* find together in a sentence, eh Red?'

Ferris wondered if the whole conversation was going to be conducted through the dog.

Mr Ezard sat down on the bench as far away from Ferris as his nose would allow.

'You owe me Ferris. I trusted you, fool that I am. Snakes in the grass have proved more reliable frankly. But sadly I have no other way of getting the result I need and now it's more than just your stinky skin that's at stake; there's a promise I can't afford to break so you need to talk fast and talk now.'

'It wasn't my fault if Mr Wolf never showed,' he whined.

'He showed alright,' said Mr Ezard, 'and the lad you told me about was following him like you said, only it wasn't the right lad.'

'Eh?' said Ferris, genuinely surprised. 'Thin lad with a shaved head?'

'Tick,' said Mr Ezard.

'And a wheezy cough?'

'Tick again.'

'Name of Jackson, with a tattooed dagger on his neck?'

'Jackson, yes, tattooed dagger, no.' Mr Ezard rubbed a weary hand over his eyes.

'Nearly turned out very nasty I can tell you. Had the lad at the safe house overnight before we realised we'd got the wrong bally boy, didn't we Red?'

Red thumped his tail but kept a clear blue eye on Ferris.

Ferris for once was lost for words. 'I don't know what to say!'

'"Sorry" would be a good start.'

''Course it's hard to say anything when you've got a dried-up throat,' rasped Ferris.

Mr Ezard sighed. He whispered something into one of Red's ears. The dog sat up straighter and gave Ferris his undivided attention.

'I'll be back in a jiff, and I want answers,' said Mr E. 'Don't even begin to contemplate departure.'

'Does he always talk like that?' said Ferris to Red.

Mr Wizard returned with a polystyrene cup of tea, as opposed to a can of anything stronger. Ferris sighed wistfully.

'It's not easy working for Mr W,' he said pouring three sachets of sugar into his drink. 'I mean he's got a nasty temper on him, really nasty.'

He sipped, coughed, and spat a lump of phlegm onto the pavement.

'Charming,' murmured Mr Ezard, moving a well-polished shoe just in time. 'Do go on.'

'And now that Mr Wolf's dealing with "livestock"…well…'

'You don't approve?' asked Mr Ezard sarcastically. 'Kidnapping, abduction and child exploitation not your thing?'

Ferris pretended not to hear.

'I mean cash, sparklers,' said Ferris, 'even the odd bit of ammunition, call me old-fashioned but that's like, fair game. But this? No! I want out and I want a deal like you said.'

'Understood,' said Mr Ezard. 'Understood and guaranteed. As long as you keep your side of the bargain and keep me informed of Mr Wolf's every move, and I mean *every*.'

'Yeah well, that's just it. I've got to set something up, soon *as* Mr W says, or I'm for it.'

'Jolly good,' said Mr Ezard, rubbing his hands together. 'I knew he'd carry on, with or without Jackson. Has he got a customer lined up?'

'So he says.'

'And he won't want to keep him waiting is my bet, yes?'

'So he says,' said Ferris again.

'And how are you going to do it? I mean no offence old boy, but no self-respecting young person is going to give you a second glance.'

'No worries.' Ferris squashed the paper coffee cup into his pocket 'Mr Wolf said I can use Roxy.'

Chapter Fourteen

At Waterloo Station sat Mynx. She called herself Mynx; no surname, just Mynx. It was her stage name, the one she was going to use when she made it big, when she got her first break. Today was just the beginning, the start of her new life

It was weird being in London, on her own. Amazing to think that from now on she would decide what she wanted to do and how she wanted to do it completely for herself.

The station was packed with people going this way and that. Like a dance, thought Mynx. Amongst the swirling crowds, some passengers stood still, staring up at the departures screen, sipping drinks from cardboard cups, waiting for their trains, looking for their friends to arrive.

Mynx was in no hurry. She settled her rucksack on a metal chair beside her. It was heavy and she needed to repack it after scrambling off the train. She had to get the underground to the Elephant and Castle, then catch a 36 as far as Peckham then text the number Stacey at school had given her. Stacey said she'd be able to stay at her mate's for as long as she needed, until she'd found her way round, got an agent or whatever.

She took out her phone and checked the number. Then she got out her purse and counted the notes tucked reassuringly inside. All her money, and some she'd been "borrowing" from around the house, came to over £200. Mynx thought it should be enough for at least a week. She'd left a note saying she was sleeping over at Stacey's. Mynx was rather pleased with that part of her plan; no way would her mum want to go to the estate where Stacey lived. Mum would rather die than be seen on the estate. Mynx knew it would be ages before she went to check. Stacey was one of the many things Mynx and her mum rowed about; "Wannabe A Film Star" TV competition was another. Mynx could have entered that competition this year, and she'd have got through she knew that, but did her mum ever listen? Did anyone?

Ferris was also at Waterloo Station.

He was looking for kids, preferably on their own. His eyes scanned the crowds as each train drew in and spilled passengers through the barriers.

A brief lull in arrivals made him take a little stroll and find a different vantage point. He was anxious not to draw attention to himself. The station employed people to keep out rough sleepers like him.

Then he saw her. She was sitting on a metal chair across from the huge screen showing breaking news, sports and adverts to entertain waiting passengers.

He watched to see if anyone came to join her. No one did. He saw her pull out her purse and count her money. He saw her put the purse and her phone in the outside pocket of her rucksack and then look up at the giant TV screen.

Perfect, thought, Ferris.

He turned towards the ticket office and raised his hand as if giving a little wave. Someone gave a nod back.

He sauntered over to towards the girl on the metal chair and waited for his chance. He didn't have long to wait.

A trailer advertising the new "Wannabe A Film Star" series caught Mynx's attention. She stared moodily at the screen, as Ferris settled himself into the vacant seat on the other side of Mynx's rucksack. Expertly and silently he dipped his hand into Mynx's rucksack pocket, slid out the phone and the purse, tucked them out of sight, yawned and stretched, then sauntered off across the station. He nodded again to the person at the ticket office as he passed.

A sports report was now showing on the screen and Mynx heaved her rucksack over her shoulder. She looked around for the underground sign. This was the bit she was nervous about; she'd never been on the underground before and couldn't help but think about bombs and stuff. She gave herself a shake and reached for her purse.

'Omigod!' said Mynx. She put her hand to her mouth and stared at where her purse had been seconds before. 'Omigod!'

Mynx dug deeper inside the pocket. No phone either. She looked all around, her legs turning to jelly as she realised what had happened.

'I don't believe this!' She was saying it out loud oblivious of the stares. 'What am I going to do?'

A woman, her face drawn and tired, touched her arm.

'Are you alright, love?' She smiled a thin smile.

Mynx clutched at the woman's arm.

'Omigod!' she said again. 'My money's been nicked and my phone and everything. What am I going to do?'

'That's awful,' said the woman. 'Let me help you, love. There's a policeman over there…'

'No not the police!' said Mynx. 'I mean to say…'

'That's OK dear,' said the woman. 'You don't want to trouble the police? I understand, trust me!'

Mynx allowed the woman to take her rucksack and lead her out of the station and off in a waiting taxi.

Ferris watched the girl talking agitatedly to the woman. Quietly, he ground the mobile phone into the floor under his foot. He slipped the notes into his pocket and threw the purse behind the coffee stall, then he made his way out of the station to the Southbank for a well-deserved drink.

The taxi stopped outside a laundrette to let Mynx and the woman out. The woman paid and Mynx stood on the pavement staring all about. This wasn't at all what she'd imagined. This place was a dump. Next to the laundrette was a Chinese Takeaway with grimy windows and a yellowing menu stuck to the door. The air was thick with cooking smells and traffic fumes, foreign voices and wailing sirens.

The woman led Mynx down an alleyway at the side of the laundrette. A cloud of steam billowed out of a side vent smelling of soap and sweat. The woman unlocked a door and Mynx followed her up an uncarpeted stair case to a small room overlooking the High Street.

'Is this London?' asked Mynx doubtfully, looking out of the window.

'What were you expecting?' asked the woman. 'A panoramic view of Tower Bridge, Houses of Parliament and Buck House all rolled into one?'

'Sorry, but I didn't think it would look so kind of ordinary.' Mynx hastily remembered her manners. 'I'm ever so grateful though really I am. I don't know what I'd have done. I'll pay you back I promise, as soon as I get a job. I'm going to be a film star.'

'Oh yes, you'll pay it all back, don't worry about that,' sighed the woman under her breath.

'Cup of tea, love?'

'Thanks. I don't know what to call you,' said Mynx, hoping the woman would ask what she was called so that she could practice her new name out loud.

'Roxy,' said the woman. 'Do you take sugar?'

'Two please, Roxy,' said Mynx. 'My name's Mynx, with a "y" by the way.'

'Whatever you say, dear,' said Roxy.

There was a sink in the corner of the room with a kettle balanced precariously on a shelf above the taps. Roxy filled the kettle and plugged it in.

'What did you say you were going to be?'

'I'm going to be a film star, or an actress anyway.'

It felt good to say it like that, to a stranger. She hoped Roxy would ask her to do one of her special voices. She did a brilliant Hermione from Harry Potter.

Instead, Roxy looked out of the window and said in a small mechanical voice, 'As a matter of fact, I can probably help you, with your career and that.'

'Honestly?' Mynx's eyes shone. 'That's brilliant! I mean what a stroke of luck us bumping into each other. What are the chances eh? It's like,' Mynx clutched her hands together, looking for the word to describe what it was like. 'Like, well, *destiny*.'

'Whatever.' Roxy poured two cups of tea and as if to change the subject she pointed to the sofa. 'That there is a bed settee. I'll get you some bedding then you can tell me all about yourself, as if I can't guess.'

Chapter Fifteen

Mitch was treated like a film star when he got back to school. Mr Barry suggested he used his experience as a basis for some extended writing. Mitch managed to include a gang of armed hoodies, a white-knuckle ride down a fast-flowing river and a heroic battle with a dangerous dog.

'Most inventive,' said Mr Barry. 'You might want to check how to spell "knife-wielding" and "Rottweiler" although frankly I doubt they'll be amongst the most commonly occurring words on the SATs spelling list.'

The novelty wore off after a week and life returned to normal.

Mitch had changed though that was for sure. He overheard his dad talking to Nan.

'Search me, Mum,' said Dad. 'Mitch is, well, back to the old Mitch somehow. It's like Annie never left us you know? And all that business with the hair? It's almost grown back. He's stopped being so, well what? Thug-like I suppose.'

Mitch tiptoed away from the kitchen and up to Nate's bedroom.

'Do you think I'm a thug?' he asked Nate.

Nate sighed and put down his guitar.

'You're a pain in the rear-end, same as always.'

He grabbed at Mitch and wrestled him onto the floor. They rolled around together until Nate managed to sit across Mitch's chest with his arms pinned behind his head.

'A thug? You're a girl, mate. A big girl. Susan! That's who you are.'

'If I'm a Susan, you're a Patsy,' said Mitch, thumping Nate across his back and kicking his legs wildly into the air.

'Give it a rest you two,' said Dad who was suddenly standing in the doorway. 'That was Nan on the phone. She's coming down at the weekend.'

'Joy! We can eat!' yelped Mitch.

'Cheeky bugger,' muttered Joe Jackson but he was smiling.

Mitch and his dad picked Nan up from the passenger ferry at Ryde.

'Good journey, Mum?' asked Dad. 'Any urges to jump off the train at inappropriate stations, that kind of thing?'

Mitch made a "humour him" face at Nan.

'Very uneventful,' said Nan, 'and I must say all the better for seeing you safe and sound.' She gave Mitch a hug. 'And the hair! Why you look almost normal!'

Mitch loved his Nan. He didn't care who knew it either. Nate had started to roll his eyes and shrug his shoulders when Nan was around like she was embarrassing him or something. And he wouldn't ever let her kiss him except when no one, and he meant absolutely no one, was looking.

That night the Jacksons went out to the Pirate Inn on the seafront for supper.

'My treat,' said Nan.

Mitch spent ages looking at the menu and trying to make up his mind.

He wanted scampi, but then there were prawns, although you didn't get chips with the prawns.

'Go on, have the prawns and an extra order of chips,' said Nan. 'It's a celebration!'

'Why?' asked Dad. 'What are we celebrating?'

'You. This.' Nan raised her glass to her three boys. 'You've made me proud. You're standing by each other and never giving up hope.'

Dad looked down at his beer. 'I don't know.'

'No she's right,' said Mitch. 'Honest Dad. Mum'll come back one day. It's going to be OK I know it is.'

Suddenly, Nate pushed his chair back from the table.

'Hello? Did we all move to La La Land? Is there any sane person left in my family? She's gone! Mum has gone. G-O-N-E in case you need me spelling it out.'

He stared angrily at them.

'Let's deal with it and do what we should have done ages ago; get—over—it!'

Nate slapped the table to emphasise what he was saying and the waitress who had arrived to take their order tiptoed tactfully away.

'Don't say that,' said Mitch. 'We don't know what's happened to her. She could be trying to get back to us right now. We can't "get over it" like you say, Nate, not without *knowing*. I mean really knowing.'

He looked hard at his dad and Nan.

'I've been thinking, I mean you never talk about how you and Mum met. We know all about you when you were little Dad, where you used to live, what school you went to, how you always wanted to be a gardener and all that but Mum...' Mitch looked at Nate. 'We don't know anything about Mum really, do we, Nate?'

Nate shrugged but Mitch didn't give up.

'I mean Dad, don't you think it's funny, us not even knowing Mum's mum?'

Dad looked away.

'You've got Nan.'

'What are you on about, Mitch?' said Nate.

'No, he's right,' said Nan to Nate. She turned and stared at Joe. 'They've got a right to know. It's time we told them the truth.'

Mitch and Nate looked at Nan and then back at Dad.

'Tell us what?' they said together.

The waitress came back.

'Are you ready to order?' she asked brightly.

Chapter Sixteen

The Pirate Inn in Ventnor was famous for its generous portions. The table was piled with plates of scampi, bread, salad and chips but no one seemed very hungry all of a sudden.

Mitch and Nate hardly dared breathe as their dad pushed away his plate and took a swig from his beer glass.

'Your mum,' said Joe. 'You want to know who her family are and where she came from? Truth is, I don't know.'

'What do you mean? You must know.' Mitch couldn't believe his dad.

'Yeah, but that's the thing. I don't. I know she was the most beautiful girl I'd ever seen. I was a bit shy to tell the truth when I was a lad, eh Mum?'
Joe looked at Nan who nodded at the boys.

'He was a bit shy, your dad, when he was little. And modest too.'

'And I wasn't what you'd call a "looker", I mean she was way out of my league and in the normal way of things…'

'You were the best-looking boy in our street!' interrupted Nan indignantly. 'See what I mean about being modest?'

'Yeah well, Mum, you would say that,' said Joe. He was looking at Nate and Mitch. 'Now if you want good looking boys,' and he gestured at his sons, 'that's what I call handsome, and clever. You get it from your mum, trust me.'

'Anyway, after I left school, I went straight to college as you know and then, in the second year, we had the chance to do work experience and I got to go to Kew Gardens.'

'What, the place with a maze near Hampton Court?' asked Mitch. 'I always wanted to go there.'

'Me and your Granddad, God bless him, were so proud,' said Nan. 'None of the others were picked, just your dad; he's always loved trees. That's what got him the place at Kew, wasn't it, Joe?'

'We know all this,' said Nate impatiently. 'You're a hippy! You love trees, hug a tree and save the world, blah blah. Skip to the bit about Mum.'

'I'm getting there Nate. As I was saying, she'd never have looked at me, no way, but as it turned out, I kind of had the advantage.'

'What do you mean?' asked Mitch.

'It was February 14th funnily enough, Valentine's day, which is how come I remember the date. I'd got in early and while I was waiting for my boss to show, I thought I'd take a stroll, maybe see if the snowdrops had started to show. There was a patch of white under one of the big old oaks they got there and I thought at first the snowdrops had grown overnight. You know like when you can't believe what you're seeing sometimes? Anyway when I got closer it wasn't snowdrops at all but a kind of tent made from a sheet of bubble wrap, the sort we used to cover the tender shrubs in the frost, and huddled up underneath it with her head on a pile of grass cuttings for a pillow was your mum.

'She was filthy dirty and her hair was like rats' tails, her face was scratched and she was, well, gorgeous.'

Nate and Mitch didn't take their eyes off Joe, but Joe was looking past them out through the window at the sea.

'That's what I mean about having the advantage. I kind of found her, you see?'

'Like in a story? You found her like in Thumbelina or something?'

'I guess Mitch, yeah, I suppose it does sound a bit weird. I don't know how she managed to hide overnight. I mean they've got dogs that sniff round and all sorts before they lock up, but somehow she managed to escape them, climbed up the tree out of sight apparently. She said she'd been eating out of the bins, or picking up bread the visitors left for the squirrels.

They're not supposed to feed the squirrels or the birds. She was like a little bird, your mum.'

Joe looked at Nan who stretched out her hand to his and held it for a moment.

'I took her back home,' he said simply. ' I didn't know what else to do with her!'

'Well, we were a bit shocked I can tell you,' said Nan. 'When she first came back with Joe, I thought we'd all catch something off her, but she scrubbed up alright eh Joe?'

'Go on then,' said Mitch. 'What happened next?'
Mitch looked at his dad and saw that his eyes were very watery, like they often were these days.

'She moved in. She just stayed. I went to Kew every day and when I got back from work, Annie would be there waiting. I was hooked.'

'Your mum was such a help,' said Nan, 'especially when Grandad got ill. I don't know how I'd have managed.'

'Every day I'd think, she'll not be there still, she'll run off again soon as she's better, but she never did…least not then…'

'But what about *her* family?' asked Mitch, interrupting, 'I mean, how come she was sleeping rough like that?'

'It's a funny thing,' said Joe. 'I often wonder about it. Sometimes a kiddy goes missing and the whole world goes mad looking for them. I mean Mitch you were getting off that train at 3:00, then you were headlines news by 10. Now why do you think that was?'

'His quick-witted and intelligent super hero brother leapt to his defence and snatched him from the jaws of death?' said Nate modestly.

Mitch snorted but Joe wasn't laughing.

'Well, actually yes, partly. All of us,' he looked at Nate and Nan, 'we'd have done anything to have found you Mitch. And if things hadn't worked out,' Joe shuddered, 'we'd have been devastated. Imagine! But it wasn't like that for Mum. She ran away when she wasn't much older than your age now Nate, only 15, and yet nobody was any the wiser.'

'What do you mean?' said Nate

74

'Well, think about it. She wasn't on the news, wasn't in the paper, not even a picture of her on a photocopied flier down in the post office! I mean to say a missing dog gets more attention. What kind of parent lets their child run off without even reporting them missing?' Joe shook his head. 'Do you know what I think? I think she was in the way. Her mum had a new bloke, and she was just in the way.'

'But what about her friends?' said Mitch 'What about her school?'

'She was about to leave school at the end of the term so…' Joe shrugged.

'And you never ever met her mum?' said Mitch. 'I've only just realised how, like well, weird that is.'

'Shouldn't we talk to Mum's mum now?' said Nate. 'She might know something.'

'And how are we going to do that?' said Joe hopelessly. 'I don't know where she is, I don't even know her name!'

'But you're married to her daughter!' protested Nate. 'You must know! What was Mum's name before she was Mrs Jackson?'

'She wouldn't tell me.' Joe shrugged. 'I didn't want to pry, didn't want to scare her away. "Just call me Roxanne," she said.'

'But she's Annie,' said Nate.

'Grandad called her that,' said Nan. 'She was very fond of him. It kind of stuck.'

'But how did you get married without knowing her surname? When you go to the registry office, you have to have a surname surely?' said Nate.

'She didn't even have a birth certificate so we couldn't get married, not properly.'

Nate and Mitch gawped, trying to make sense of what Joe was saying.

'So she's not Mrs Jackson? You and Mum aren't married?'

'You've been pretending to be married then?' said Nate.

'It's only a name. She *calls* herself Mrs Jackson…it's easier that way. What does it matter?'

75

'I don't believe this,' said Nate. 'You don't know *anything* about her life before you met her? I mean weren't you even curious?'

Joe was suddenly angry.

'Well, did *you* ever ask her? Did you ever say to your mum, what was it like when you were a girl? Did you ever even ask her about her mum or her dad? No! 'Course not. Too wrapped up in yourselves. It never occurred to either of you why you've only got one Nan, did it?'

'I suppose I thought she was dead,' said Mitch.

'Would she have told us even if we *had* asked?' said Nate defensively although inside he felt ashamed.

'Who knows? She never let me get close to that side of her life.'

Joe blew his nose and drained the last drop of beer from his glass.

'When she came to live with us at your Nan and Grandad's, she had nothing, did she, Mum? Only the filthy clothes she was wearing. And a bin liner with a few bits in.'

'Well,' said Nan, 'that's true; except, of course, there was the jacket.'

Chapter Seventeen

'So,' said Ferris to Mr Wolf, 'when do you want to take a look?'

'Where is the item at the moment?'

'I've got her at Roxy's,' said Ferris.

'Ah!' said Mr Wolf. 'Where would we be without Roxy? Does Roxy know about our new line of business?'

Ferris shook his head. 'She thinks she's getting another runner, just like normal. She don't know nothing about this new line of work. She won't be happy neither so best not mention it.'

'Do I look like I need advice on staff management?' snapped Mr Wolf. 'Roxy does what she's told same as always.'

'Of course, of course,' said Ferris hastily, anxious to keep on the right side of the boss. 'It's just that since she's been back...'

'What?' said Mr Wolf. 'Since she's been back... What were you going to say?'

'Well, she's changed. I mean she's not the Roxy I remember.'

'That was 15 years ago, more if you think. Even you've begun to lose some of your good looks Ferris.' Mr Wolf chuckled at his joke. 'No she's got older but she's still the same old Roxy. That's why I got her back. We need someone we can trust, someone we can rely on, someone who won't dare let us down.'

Mr Wolf scratched his chin thoughtfully. 'I'll come and take a butcher's, shall we say Tuesday? Unless you've got anything pressing in your diary?'

Roxy put a cup of tea down on the floor by the sofa bed and stared at the sleeping girl.

Mynx! she thought to herself. *More like Alice, or Sarah but never Mynx.*

The girl turned over and her mouth fell open to show a set of perfect white teeth. Her coat was spread over the blanket Roxy had found for her; it was lined in pink silk.

Someone will be missing you, thought Roxy. She bent down to gently shake her awake.

'Wake up, Mynx, or whoever you are,' she said. 'Tea's up!'

***

Ferris and Mr Ezard sat together on a bench looking at the Thames. Behind them, a man, sprayed from top to bottom in white paint, stood as still as a statue, only moving when a passer-by put money in his upturned hat.

'Begging as an art form!' sighed Ferris. 'I've got no chance of making a decent wage.'

'You're not wrong there,' said Mr Ezard. 'So, what have we got?'

'I'm meeting up with Mr W at Roxy's,' said Ferris. 'She's looking after a very promising piece of live bait. It's all arranged for Tuesday, 6:00.'

'Then what happens?' asked Mr Ezard.

'You give me my reward, a nice clean slate, and we all live happily ever after.'

'Apart from that,' sighed Mr Ezard, 'what happens to the girl and this, who did you say, Roxy?'

'Roxy? She's one of Mr Wolf's best runners, been doing it for years on and off, well more off over the last few years, yeah, streuth, it's got to be fifteen years now I think about it, but she's back now and on the case 24/7. And the girl, well Mr W reckons she'll be just the job for this big shot customer he knows. Roxy's not going to like it I'm telling you now.'

Mr Ezard looked sharply at Ferris.

'You mean she doesn't know Wolf's taken up kidnapping for a hobby? She hasn't twigged what he's up to? What does she think, that he's setting up a bally Ballet school?'

'Be fair, Mr E,' said Ferris. 'I mean to say it's one thing to be taking the odd package of dodgy fivers stuffed in your handbag from x to y, but we're into a whole new ball game here, and only Mr W knows the rules.'

'So Roxy's role in all this is what exactly?' asked Mr Ezard, 'Just so that I can be clear.'

'She's like a housekeeper I suppose. I mean she does the odd run, sure, like we all do. I mean years ago she was Mr Wolf's star turn so to speak. The stuff they shifted!' Ferris rummaged in his pocket for his tobacco and began to roll a straggly looking cigarette. ''Course it was easier then, before all that scanning nonsense at airports. Not that they ever took me. I've never been further than Brighton.'

'What do you mean "star turn"?'

'Well, she was so young, of course, when Mr W first met her. He was young too, you might almost say glamorous. I first met Roxy the night before she was on her way to South Africa. She thought they were going on holiday...'

'Whereas in fact, what was it? A run?' enquired Mr Ezard.

Ferris nodded. 'Diamonds. Roxy swore blind she never knew. He was always buying her stuff was Mr W, you know clothes and that, stuff young girls go for, and then he got her a jacket like his, the very same one he still wears. Almost the exact match it was; leather with a picture of a wolf howling at the moon on the back.'

'The wolf jacket eh,' said Mr Ezard to himself. 'I thought as much.'

'Yeah. It was bulky, flashy, and pretty much made to order. Now another reason Roxy was so perfect for the run was she and Mr W were more or less the same size. He was slight and wiry, she was straggly and tall, and the jackets were pretty much interchangeable which, of course, was the point.'

'In what sense, the point?'

'Well, he hid the goods in the lining of *one* of the jackets. First time they came back from Cape Town, Roxy just thought she was holding his jacket when he got searched at customs, then Wolfy made sure to swap the jackets when they asked to look in all the pockets. The customs geezers searched the same *empty* jacket twice. Roxy never noticed, never knew nothing until later on, much later.'

'And you know all this, how exactly?'

Ferris shifted uncomfortably and picked a wet strand of tobacco off his lower lip. 'I'm not proud of my career Mr E, you know that. Otherwise, why would I be working for you like this? I'm not about to incriminate myself here am I?'

Mr Ezard gritted his teeth and moved his face uncomfortably closer to Ferris.

'This isn't about thieving a few bangles like the good old days, in case you haven't noticed. This, you revolting snitch, is about dealing in human misery, buying and selling people, *children* for pity's sake. Your man Wolf is no better than a predator, an animal, living off human flesh. You want out, and I want rid. Stop whining Ferris and keep talking.'

Chapter Eighteen

'Nice coat,' said Roxy after Mynx had got up and had some breakfast.

'S'alright, I suppose,' said Mynx.

'Looks expensive and all.'

'Yeah well, my dad's guilt-trip can be pretty lucrative!' Mynx laughed without any warmth. 'He's got a new family now, so I expect that's one funding stream which is about to dry up. Not that I give a monkey's…the next time he sees me will be from the flat screen side of a TV.'

'Listen to me a minute,' said Roxy. She sat down in front of Mynx. 'How old are you?'

'None of your business! Just because you helped me out yesterday doesn't mean you've got a right…'

'No, of course not, I'm sorry,' said Roxy, 'it's just that thirteen-year-olds are…'

'I'm FOURteen actually,' said Mynx, putting her hand to her mouth when she realised what she'd said.

'Quite. You need to go home, Mynx, you really do. I know.'

'What do you mean you *know*? How can you *know*? Have you any idea what it's like being invisible? I mean nobody ever listens to me, nobody. I don't think anyone in my house has like a single clue as to even who I am. I bet they don't even know what *music* I like.'

'Outrageous.'

'See?' Mynx pouted, 'they'll be sorry though, I promise you that.'

'Oh I'm sure of it,' said Roxy. 'The trouble is, so will you be…sorry that is.'

Roxy sighed. 'You remind me of another girl I used to know; I knew her very well about sixteen years ago it would be now. We lost touch for a long time, but now I'm afraid she's back.'

'Why are you afraid?' asked Mynx.

'I don't like her,' said Roxy. 'Oh I don't mean I don't like *you*. We don't know each other, do we? Not yet anyway. No it's just what you're doing. It's not right. This other girl, she thought she could make it on her own, like you think you can, and she got into a very bad place, really, really bad.' Roxy shuddered. 'She's not far from that place again, after everything she tried to do to keep away. It creeps up on you though, pulls you back in.'

'What are you talking about?' asked Mynx. 'You're not making any sense.'

'No. Well.'

The doorbell rang and made Roxy give a little start. She went to the window, pulled back the curtain, and peered down into the street.

'Ferris,' she said.

'Who's Ferris?' Mynx peered over Roxy's shoulder. 'Yuk. He looks revolting.'

'Oh he's harmless,' said Roxy. 'It's not him you got to watch out for, it's…'

The doorbell rang again, more urgently.

'Better see what he wants,' said Roxy. 'You stay here.'

Mynx looked down on the street from the window. She saw the dosser bloke pacing around outside the laundrette. She saw Roxy join him. They both looked up at the window and Mynx gave a little wave. They talked for ages. Roxy stepped back a few paces shaking her head and Ferris seemed to be trying to reason with her, then he shrugged and raised his hands as if to say he didn't care and shuffled off.

Mynx waited for Roxy to come back upstairs. Her face was a sickly shade of white.

'I can't do this,' she said simply. 'I can't do this anymore.'

'Do what?' Mynx waited for Roxy to speak. Instead, she sat down heavily on the bed settee. She fiddled with her hair, twisting a lock into a knot around her finger. After a moment, she seemed to make up her mind; she took a deep breath.

'I'm not what you think, Mynx.'

She pulled at another twist of hair and made another tangled knot.

'I didn't just happen to pick you up yesterday out of the goodness of my heart, do you get me?'

Mynx shook her head as if to say she didn't get her at all.

'Your phone? Your purse? It was a set-up, you stupid kid, you've been grabbed.'

'What do you mean grabbed?' Mynx's face was turning the same colour as Roxy's.

'Grabbed, captured, kidnapped, whatever you want to call it—me too in some ways. We're in this together except that you are the innocent victim whereas me…I'm in it up to here.' Roxy drew an invisible line around her neck.

'Thing is,' Roxy got up and held Mynx by the shoulders, staring anxiously into her face, 'it just got complicated. You've got to get out. Now. Before it's too late.'

Mynx's eyes filled and her mouth trembled. She stared at Roxy, unable to understand.

'Get out?' said Mynx. 'Don't you want to help me then?'

'That's exactly what I'm trying to do Mynx.'

'But you said you knew people in the film industry…people who could help me be famous.'

Roxy walked over to the shabby armchair with its thread-bare cover.

'What did you think? Look around you. Does this look like a place someone who knows famous people might live?'

'But I thought…' Mynx stopped. What had she thought? Suddenly, she wanted to go home.

'Can I call Mum?'

'Yeah, wouldn't that be great if we could just call our mums,' said Roxy bitterly. 'I wanted to call mine when I was your age but she'd moved away, found a new bloke. I wanted to say I'd made a mistake and ask if I could come home. I'd got the big sorry speech all worked out, plucked up the courage to ring; but the number was unobtainable, just like her.'

'But my mum won't do that to me,' said Mynx. 'She loves me. She'll want me back I know she will.'

'You've changed your tune,' said Roxy. 'But don't worry Mynx, I'll get you out of this, I promise.'

The doorbell rang again. This time Roxy really jumped. She looked around as if searching for somewhere to hide.

'If that's Wolf...'

'Who's Wolf?' said Mynx sensing the fear in Roxy's voice.

'Lucky you don't know, believe me. Just have a peep out the window Mynx.'

'Some bloke with a dog,' said Mynx.

'I don't know a bloke with a dog,' said Roxy as the doorbell rang longer this time.

'Let me have a look.'

The man caught her eye before she had a chance to drop the curtain.

'Damn, he's seen me,' said Roxy. She looked at Mynx again. 'I'd better go and find out what he wants, but when I've got rid of him we'll sort this out. Properly.'

Chapter Nineteen

Mr Wolf always went to the gym on Monday, every week without fail. It was quiet on Monday, which was just as he liked it. He used it not only to keep fit, but also to do a little business from time to time.

There was a notice board for members, a place where people put up information about forthcoming events or items for sale. It had proved a very convenient way of communicating with one of Mr Wolf's best clients. He never used his home phone for business and didn't trust his mobile. He certainly kept well clear of the internet when contacting customers. He was in awe of his computer and used it for pleasure only, buying things for his collection or researching his hobby. Mind you that had led to a wicked bit of luck a few months back. Mr Wolf chuckled and rubbed his whiskery chin as he remembered the day he'd found Roxy. Who would have guessed?

He'd been surfing for a hunting gun, something he could put on the wall next to his wolf skin. He'd meant to type "hunting" into the search engine but he made a mistake and for some reason typed hunt*er*. Before he'd realised his error, he saw an entry which caught his eye, "Head Hunter". He'd clicked. Imagine! Just a little click! And there she was. Little old Roxanne after all this time, standing like goody two shoes outside a hairdresser's shop, her new hairdressers shop that she'd called Head-Hunter, like it was an invitation sent just for him! There she was, posing and simpering for the camera. He read the article and discovered she was married, had two boys, and lived in a backwater on an island off the south coast.

He'd made her a visit and a very special offer. Yes, the Internet was a most useful invention.

The use of the notice board in the gym however had been one of his own inventions. He pulled a little card from his wallet and pinned it to the board. It was handwritten and said quite simply

Pedigree livestock now available for inspection Tuesday 9:00 a.m.

***

Mr Ezard sat back in the shabby armchair and beamed. Red thumped his tail.

'So, Mrs Jackson! Thank you so much for agreeing to see me.'

Nobody spoke.

Mr Ezard continued. 'It is Mrs Jackson? Mrs Roxanne Jackson? We seem to have made a habit of getting the wrong Jackson, Red and I.'

Roxy was sitting on the bed settee in a state of shock.

'How did you know?' she said faintly. 'No one knows, only Wolfie.'

Mr Ezard slipped his hand inside his jacket's pocket and pulled out a battered newspaper clipping.

'*Nick Nack, Mitch is Back*,' he read from the paper. 'Have a look Mrs Jackson.'

Roxy read it. 'But that's my Mitch!'

'Yes, but don't worry they're all back safe and sound somewhere on the Isle of Wight. Nice family.'

'But how did you know? I mean how come you found me?'

'A bit of luck my dear. It was all about the jacket you see?'

Roxy blinked. 'What jacket?'

'*The* jacket. The one I think you stuffed in the shed at Joe's mum's? Full of useful pockets with a rather distinctive design?'

'How do you know about that?' said Roxy.

'If your boys, fine fellows I must say, hadn't been fighting over who would get to wear the jacket, *your* jacket, Mrs Jackson senior wouldn't have shaved Mitch's head. I wouldn't have mistaken the shaven Mitch for someone else entirely and thus, belatedly, heard all about your disappearance. You see I've been after our Wicked Wolf for many months and done a lot of homework. I knew he'd had an accomplice, years ago, a young girl who disappeared into thin air.'

'Are you some sort of policeman?' said Roxy interrupting sharply.

'Well, *some* sort I suppose,' said Mr Ezard. 'After all, how else would a chap like me know a chap like Ferris?'

'You know Ferris?' said Roxy in disbelief.

'Certainly I do. Very useful source is Ferris. Ferris told me how that young girl, the one who disappeared fifteen years ago and is now a young woman, had somewhat mysteriously reappeared a mere two months since. I checked the Isle of Wight police records and matched up some dates.

Ferris' description was just like the one your Joe, Mr Jackson, had given the police. I thought it was worth coming to see for myself.'

Mynx was staring at Roxy. 'What's he on about?'

Roxy took a deep breath, like a swimmer about to plunge into a pool.

'Oh what does it matter? I'm in so deep now...' She held Mynx's hands.

'You know that girl I was telling you about? The one I didn't like much?'

Mynx nodded

'That was me. I ran away, like you, came to London looking for adventure and I found it, oh yes I found it alright.'

'Enter the big bad wolf?' suggested Mr Ezard

Roxy laughed but not like anything was funny.

'Wolfie, yeah. He was alright at first. Bought me stuff; that jacket for a start, took me to fancy clubs, we even went abroad. 'Course that was the point.'

'What was the point?' said Mynx her eyes glued to Roxy.

'Always going on holidays,' continued Roxy as if she hadn't heard. 'We went to places I couldn't have imagined someone like me ever going to; Amsterdam, Bangkok, Cape Town, the Caribbean, all over the place.'

'Yes I bet you did,' said Mr Ezard, partly to himself.

'Little by little I twigged what was going on. He was using me! Using me to carry all his trade, through customs, past policemen. I was taking all the risks.'

'What, like smuggling? Diamonds and stuff?' Mynx was agog.

'And the rest,' said Roxy. 'He reckoned that if I was the one to get caught it would go easier for me 'cos I was so young. But we weren't ever caught.

'Then one day I wanted out. Told him I'd had enough. He got nasty then, really nasty so I ran away again.' She felt for a tissue up her sleeve. 'I'm good at that.'

Mynx went and sat next to Roxy on the settee and put a hand on her knee.

'I went to Kew Gardens, in London. I'd been there once, years ago with my Nan.

'I thought I'd be safe, didn't think he'd look for me there. Give myself time to think.'

'But why didn't you just go back home?' said Mynx. 'To your real home I mean?'

'I told you,' said Roxy. 'I ran once when things were getting bad with Wolfie. Number unobtainable. They'd moved on and left me behind, like I was left over rubbish.'

'But that's terrible,' said Mynx. She reached for Roxy's hand. 'What happened next?'

'My Joe,' said Roxy. 'He sort of found me, hiding in the park. Took me in, him and his parents, looked after me. Then we got the chance to go to the Isle of Wight when Joe got a job at the Botanic Gardens. I started to breathe again, stopped looking behind me. It's a small place, you get to feel like you belong you know? And then, of course, we had the boys. I thought I was safe, I thought we all were.'

She dabbed at her eyes.

'Anyway it's been nearly eight weeks since he turned up, Wolfie, out of nowhere. He rang me at the shop. It gave me such a shock. He said I had to meet him the next day, early. Said he needed me back working for him, and if I didn't come he'd tip off the police, and, even worse, he'd tell Joe and the kids.'

Roxy was really crying now. Mynx put her arms around her.

'They never knew, see?' said Roxy. 'I never told them. But Wolfie said I'd go to prison 'cos of what I'd done all those years ago. I couldn't bear it; couldn't bear to think what it would do to the boys; the shame of it all.'

Roxy shook her head as if to get rid of the thought. 'It's breaking my heart, not being with them; it's really breaking my heart.'

'Let me get you some water,' said Mynx. 'Or a cup of tea?'

'You're a good girl Mynx,' said Roxy. 'You've got to get out, get home while you still can.'

'But what about you?' said Mynx.

'What about me?' said Roxy bitterly. 'Nothing's changed. Wolfie would shop me to the police, like he said; only this time it'll be worse. I mean I hate to think what he was going to do...' She shook her head again.

'Ah,' said Mr Ezard. 'That's the thing you see. There's really not much to "shop" as you put it. We already know.'

'What, everything?' Roxy glanced at Mynx. 'You mean to say you know what Wolfie's new business is?'

Mr Ezard nodded.

'That's great that is!' said Roxy angrily. 'So I'm the last person to know! And what were you going to do about her?'

She turned to Mynx.

'I promise you Mynx, I had no idea about any of this. I thought he just wanted another runner, like I was you know? I mean I wasn't proud of what we did, back there at the station, but I wouldn't have let him hurt you honest I wouldn't. You do believe me don't you?'

Mynx and Roxy hugged each other again, and this time Mynx was crying too.

'It's alright,' she said. 'The police will sort it all out eh?' She looked at Mr Ezard.

'Not enough proof I'm afraid,' said Mr Ezard. 'He's been very cunning, our Mr Wolf has, very cunning indeed.'

'Wait a minute,' said Roxy, drying her eyes and looking suspiciously at him. 'You and Ferris have got some plan all worked out haven't you?'

Mr Ezard shrugged modestly.

'Well,' said Roxy angry again. 'Don't go planning on Mynx. It's too dangerous.'

'Hold on!' said Mynx. 'Don't I get a say in this? What kind of plan?'

Mr Ezard rubbed his chin but said nothing.

'I mean what?' said Mynx. 'Come on tell me. What sort of proof do you need?'

'It doesn't matter Mynx,' said Roxy. 'Whatever proof they need won't involve you.'

'Ah well no, of course not,' said Mr Ezard looking sideways at Mynx, 'at least not if you don't want it to…'

'But I do want it to!' said Mynx. She let go of Roxy. 'Don't you see? We've got the chance to put this right, haven't we Mr Ezard? I reckon you need a piece of live bait, a lamb to tempt a wolf sort of thing? And that's me yeah? Cool! A starring role at last but this time for real!'

Chapter Twenty

It was Tuesday. For once in his life, Ferris managed a shower at the hostel and a shave. He even washed his hair. Today it was all going to change. Today was make or break day. He whistled a jaunty tune as he made his way to Roxy's flat.

Mynx and Roxy had been ready for ages. Roxy had her bags packed and ready in the bedroom, Mynx was sitting meekly on the bed settee.

'Do you need to go over this again?' asked Roxy, sitting down beside Mynx.

Mynx shook her head. 'No it's OK. I think I've got it. Let me see, we wait for that revolting Ferris and Mr Wolf to come. I act like I'm all excited about this screen test he's going to get me. Mr Wolf will take us both off in the taxi to meet this geezer right?' She suddenly looked panicked. 'S'pose Mr Wolf won't let you come in the taxi?'

'No he will. That's my job now,' said Roxy. 'See, he reckons that as long as a friendly woman's around you won't get suspicious. Let's face it, you trusted me didn't you, but would you have trusted Ferris?'

'No way!' said Mynx.

'Well, compared with Mr Wolf, Ferris is a pussycat. And he hates a scene Wolfie does. He'll want me to come along so that you stay calm.'

'Whatever. One thing, are you sure Mr Ezard is up to this? I mean, no offence to him, seemed like a nice bloke, but that business with your son. He messed that up big time.'

'We've got to trust someone Mynx,' said Roxy.

The white van had HDN written across the back doors. Inside, Red and Mr Ezard were waiting patiently. Mr Ezard was wearing some clear thick-framed glasses and a tee shirt with the words "Home Delivery Network" printed across the back.

'Rather appropriate,' he smiled to himself admiring his disguise. 'Home delivering is exactly what this operation is all about.'

He had tested his radio control, ensuring that the back-up was in place. He'd checked that a pile of parcels were ready on the passenger seat along with some documentation and a fake ID card, then he'd settled himself down in his seat to wait.

***

On the Isle of Wight, Mitch waved goodbye to Dad. Dad always dropped both the boys outside the school gate. He couldn't bear to let them catch the bus, not yet. Nate moaned but was secretly relieved.

The wind was nippy and made Nate shiver.

'Why don't you wear your jacket?' asked Mitch.

Nate shrugged. 'Dunno.'

'Is it because of what happened?'

'Ye-es,' said Nate, 'but it's not just that.'

'What then?'

'I feel different when I wear it, like it changes the way I feel?'

'In a good way?' asked Mitch.

'No man!' Nate sucked his teeth like a rude boy.

'But when Nan gave it to you that weekend we went up, you said you loved it.'

'Do you know what, I did love that jacket at first, then by the next day I don't know I was feeling like moody you know?'

'And the rest,' muttered Mitch.

'I didn't realise for ages but I feel lighter somehow without it...'

'For real do you mean?'

Nate glanced at his brother to check that he wasn't laughing.

'Yes for real if you must know, and before you ask, no, I have no idea why.'

***

Outside the launderette Ferris was waiting. He kept glancing at the white van, and then up at the window above the Chinese take away. He could see two anxious faces.

A mini cab stopped.

The van driver put away his sandwich and flask.

The curtains in the flat tweaked.

'Lovely morning,' said Ferris hurrying to open the door for Mr Wolf.

'It might be, I'll let you know,' said Mr Wolf. 'Are we going up?' He nodded towards the flat.

'No need,' said Ferris. 'They'll be down as soon as I ring. You won't be disappointed Mr W. Trust me, she's a looker.'

Mr Wolf told the mini-cab driver to wait and allowed Ferris to ring the doorbell.

'This is it Mynx,' said Roxy squeezing her hand. 'All set?'

'It's Lucy,' said Mynx in a little voice. 'I'm not really called Mynx at all.'

Roxy looked at Mynx/Lucy. She seemed so small, swamped in her beautiful coat with the silk lining and weighed down with her rucksack.

'You're a star whatever you're called, never mind all that Wannabes nonsense.' said Roxy and she hugged Lucy hard. 'We're going to get through this and then go back home. For good.'

From the white Home Delivery Network van, Mr Ezard watched as Lucy and Roxy stood on the pavement. He saw Mr Wolf walk round the girl and nod his approval at Ferris. He saw Ferris turn up his collar as arranged. Mr Ezard started up the engine and waited until Roxy, Lucy and Mr Wolf got into the cab and set off towards the West End. Mr Ezard slipped into first gear and followed, making a thumbs up sign to Ferris who watched until both vehicles were out of sight.

Chapter Twenty-One

The cab stopped at the gym and let out the passengers. Mr Ezard pulled in over the road and got out a parcel. He wound down the window.

'Right old chap,' he said to Red. 'Paws crossed eh. And keep an ear out in case things get interesting.'

Red whined in a low tone and settled down to wait.

Mr Wolf ushered Lucy and Roxy into the gym. It was a very posh members-only sort of place with potted ferns in the foyer and leather seats. The woman behind the desk looked up and recognised Mr Wolf straight away.

'Good morning, sir!' she said politely. 'Have you got a booking?'

'I'm meeting someone, that is *we* are,' said Mr Wolf. 'Can you ring through to the sauna suite? He's expecting us.'

'Certainly, I shan't keep you a moment.'

They sat on the leather seats, Roxy feeling increasingly nervous.

'It's ever so nice of you to arrange all this,' said Lucy. 'I mean you don't even know me!'

Roxy had to admire Lucy. She was playing a very convincing role.

Lucy went on. 'And will this man you told me about, this man I haven't met, really want to give me a part in a film?'

'I said so didn't I?' snarled Mr Wolf forgetting for a moment not to frighten the girl. Hastily he cleared his throat. 'You don't know me very well my dear but I say what I mean and mean what I say.'

Lucy smiled, but Roxy could see that Mr Wolf's manner had given her a shock.

The front door swung open and a tall man in glasses and wearing a tee shirt with HDN written across the front came over to the counter. He put a large parcel on the desk.

'A very good morning to you, young lady,' he said to the receptionist. 'Care to sign for this parcel?'

'What is it?' she asked frostily.

'That's for you to discover I dare say,' he replied, 'but not until you've signed on the dotted line.'

The girl sighed.

'Give it over here then,' she said.

Another door opened behind her and three men walked into the foyer. Two were large and wore earpieces. The one in the middle was smaller, plumper, and sleeker.

The deliveryman fumbled in his pocket for his phone and, smiling apologetically at the receptionist, appeared to make a call.

Mr Wolf stood up and nudged Lucy to do the same. He stepped forward and shook the plump man's hand.

The plump man narrowed his eyes and looked Lucy up and down. He smiled an unconvincing smile.

'Very nice,' he said to Mr Wolf, beckoning to one of the large men to come forward.

The large man put his hand in his jacket and pulled out an envelope, which he passed to Mr Wolf.

The deliveryman folded up his phone and stepped forward.

'Good morning, gentlemen. I wonder if we might have a word.'

He stood in front of the four men keeping Lucy and Roxy behind him.

Mr Wolf stuffed the envelope out of sight and looked anxiously towards the exit.

'A word?' said the plump man. 'Why on earth would I want a word with you?'

'Well now,' said Mr Ezard to the deliveryman, pretending to think about the question, 'let's start with that envelope you've just handed to this gentleman here.'

Mr Ezard indicated Mr Wolf who was already trying to slink off.

'I hope you realise you're trespassing,' said the plump man. 'This is a private club and that goes for any business we might choose to do here; private. Understand?'

He flicked his fingers at the two large men who stepped towards Mr Ezard squaring their shoulders.

'Shall I call the manager?' said the receptionist, a finger ready on the keypad.

'I think you'd better,' said the plump man. 'He won't want any trouble. After all, I've been a member here for fourteen years.'

'What a coincidence!' said Mr Ezard jauntily, 'You became a member the year this young lady was born.'

The plump man went pale. 'Who did you say you were?'

'I didn't, but the name's Ezard.' He took out a warrant card from his jacket and held it up to the plump man. 'I'm afraid you're nicked.'

As he said this, Mr Wolf was backing towards the door. Mr Ezard whistled through two fingers in his mouth and Red leapt out of the car and stood growling out in the street, guarding the exit.

Mr Wolf spun round to see what was making the noise.

'It's that ruddy dog!' he said. 'I knew he was trouble when I saw him that day, that day when I went to get Jackson.'

He looked at Mr Ezard and then at Roxy. 'This is a set-up! You can't get away with this. You've got no proof.'

'This time I've got all the proof I need, old chap.'
Mr Ezard tapped the phone he'd just used for filming. He looked at the plump man and his minders.

'I do hope you haven't booked yourselves a workout session; we've got the gym surrounded. Mind you there'll be plenty of bars where you're going, more vertical than parallel...'

***

Mitch hated homework. He took out the dog-eared photocopied sheet and stared at it gloomily. "Similes". He had to fill in the missing words. Mr Barry said he'd give extra points for anyone who came up with something really original.

1.   As shy as a…

What was shy? A mouse? Sally Evans was shy. Better not. Mitch wrote "mouse" over the dots.

2.   As cunning as a…

What about a fox? No, everyone would have that. A baddie? Not really. A wolf?

Mitch put down his pen and frowned. The wolf jacket was still bothering him. He and his Nan had talked about it on the phone the other day.

'Why did you keep it all that time, Nan?' he'd asked.

'I don't know, pet,' she'd said. 'I mean it was the only thing your mum had with her. Doesn't Nate like it then?'

'I'm not sure. He said it made him feel kind of heavy.'

'Well it's lined, of course, and leather isn't light after all.'

'I don't think he meant that sort of heavy. More kind of depressed?'

'Oh, I see. No news I suppose?'

Mitch knew what Nan meant.

'No news Nan.'

'Don't give up on her pet,' said Nan.

Mitch hadn't given up. He had faith in Mr Wizard.

3.   As precious as…

That was easy. Mitch wrote "*a dearest wish*". He sighed and rubbed it out; he wrote "*a necklace*" instead. He didn't want Jason thinking he'd gone soft.

***

The shuttle bus went from Shanklin railway station to Ventnor and back every hour. As Mitch was writing "a dearest wish", the sole passenger was getting off the bus and walking up Ventnor high street.

She passed a hairdresser's shop with "Closed Until Further Notice" written on the door. She stopped and reread it. Her eyes shone. *Not shut for good then*, she thought to herself.

She walked up the hill as far as South Street, and turned slowly into the road.

She passed the familiar houses and got nearer and nearer to number 12.

She rang the bell and held her breath.